ANDI UNEXPECTED

Other books by Amanda Flower

Appleseed Creek Mystery Series

A Plain Death

A Plain Scandal

A Plain Disappearance

India Hayes Mystery Series

Maid of Murder

Murder in a Basket

Amish Quilt Shop Mystery Series

(writing as Isabella Alan)

Murder, Plain and Simple

AN ANDI BOGGS NOVEL

ANDI UNEXPECTED

AMANDA FLOWER

ZONDER**kidz**

ZONDERKIDZ

Andi Unexpected
Copyright © 2013 by Amanda Flower

This title is also available as a Zondervan ebook.
Visit www.zondervan.com/ebooks

Requests for information should be addressed to:
Zonderkidz, 5300 Patterson Ave SE, Grand Rapids, Michigan 49530

ISBN 978-0-310-73701-8

Editor: Kim Childress
Cover illustration: Chris Coady
Cover design: Cindy Davis

Printed in the United States of America

13 14 15 16 17 18 19 /DCI/ 19 18 17 16 15 14 13 12 11 10 9 8 7 6 5 4 3 2

For my brother, Andy

Mr. Cragmeyer's knuckles turned white. He held the steering wheel in a death grip as the Oldsmobile crested yet another rolling hill. His gray buzzcut stood on end as if electrified, and his shoulders hunched forward. There was no other traffic on the country road. The last mode of transportation we'd seen was an Amish horse and buggy, and that was about forty minutes ago.

Mrs. Cragmeyer turned around in the passenger seat and looked at us. She clutched the headrest with one speckled hand. Her fingernails were filed to a point and painted a translucent baby pink. "Now, girls," she said, holding her seat belt away from her throat. "If you don't like living with your Aunt Amelie, you're always welcome to come back and stay with Mr. Cragmeyer and me. We have plenty of room."

My sister Bethany, who was listening to her iPod and drawing in her sketchbook, had stopped listening to Mrs. Cragmeyer hours ago. I wished I had her ability to shut out the world. Even when I was deep in the midst of a science experiment, I couldn't help but notice what was happening around me. But when Bethany drew, nothing but her paper and pencil existed.

I wondered how Mr. Cragmeyer felt about his wife's open invitation. He hadn't said two words since we left Cuyahoga Falls, and he'd said even less than that during the past few weeks that we'd been living in their house while we finished up the school year.

Mrs. Cragmeyer turned back around and sniffed, "That aunt of yours is too irresponsible to raise children."

The cow pastures and fields gave way to houses and a suspect gas station. Mrs. Cragmeyer read aloud from a folksy road sign as we drove past, "Welcome to Killdeer, Ohio! Home of Your Friends!" Mrs. Cragmeyer snorted. Underneath images of frolicking Amish children, another line read: MICHAEL PIKE UNIVERSITY—1¾ MILES.

On the outskirts of town, we drove past the abandoned building that once housed the Michael Pike Bottling Company. It was an old, flat-faced brick structure with tall cooling towers and brick chimneys. A new sign stuck out from the side of building: KILLDEER HISTORICAL SOCIETY AND BOTTLING MUSEUM.

We drove down Center Street through the heart of Killdeer, past Betty Anne Curlers Beauty Parlor, McDonald's, Hot Cross Bakers, and the gates of

Michael Pike University. Mr. Cragmeyer consulted the driving directions he'd taped to the dashboard of the Oldsmobile. He claimed he didn't trust a GPS or any other "newfangled" technology.

Without warning, he made a sharp turn off Center Street and onto Dunlap Avenue.

I slid across the backseat and bumped into Bethany, who gruffly pushed me away. "You made me mess up," she snapped, erasing the tiny stray line on her paper.

Oh, so she can *talk. That's a relief.* Bethany hadn't said a word to me all day.

"Mr. Cragmeyer!" Mrs. Cragmeyer exclaimed, "*Do* be careful. There are children in the car."

Mr. Cragmeyer grunted and squinted at the house numbers along the street. He couldn't have missed my aunt's house if he tried. Amelie stood in the middle of the fourth driveway on the right-hand side of the street, jumping up and down in front of a two-story yellow house with white shutters and a wide front porch. Even though my grandma had died when I was seven, I could still see her sitting on that porch, rocking away in her white rocker. The yellow paint was now peeling, but the rocker was still there.

Amelie's multicolored peasant skirt swished back and forth over her bare feet and legs as she hurried over to the car.

Mrs. Cragmeyer muttered something under her breath, but the only words I caught were "crazy" and "hippy."

A small smile formed on my lips. *We'll be okay now,* I thought. *Not perfect, but okay.* I'd happily take "okay" after living with Mrs. Cragmeyer who constantly told me to either stand up straight, not talk with my mouth full, or cross my legs like a lady. Of course, Bethany never received any of this advice because Bethany is beautiful. In Mrs. Cragmeyer's world, that trait granted you a pass.

My sister is tall and thin like me, but our similarities end there. Bethany has naturally tan skin, bright blue eyes, and long, thick blond hair. I, on the other hand, have pale skin that burns even in February, undistinguishable hazel eyes, and pink hair. My mom used to tell me that I was a strawberry blond, and that one day I would love my hair color. But let's face it: The hair looks pink—especially in the sunlight. As if that weren't bad enough, I also have braces … and not the cool invisible kind either.

I smiled as Amelie continued to hop from foot to foot on the white gravel driveway. With her purple cat eye glasses, wild blond curls, and big feet, Aunt Amelie didn't care that I wasn't pretty like Bethany. She was family—the only family Bethany and I had left.

Silent Mr. Cragmeyer rolled the Olds to a stop in Amelie's driveway. I could hear the gravel crunch beneath the tires as they sank into the damp earth. Not able to wait another second, Amelie pounced and threw open my car door. She pulled me out of the vehicle by the arm, barely giving me time to release the seat belt, and crushed me in a tight hug. She smelled like fresh pears and salsa. "Andi! I'm so glad you're finally here. How was the trip? Did you see any cows on the drive? About a thousand, right? Not exactly a booming metropolis out here, is it?"

Before I could answer any of those questions, Amelie let me go and crushed Bethany in an equally tight hug before slamming her with a half-dozen random questions. My sister held her sketchbook close to her chest as though she needed to protect it from our aunt.

Amelie moved on to Mrs. Cragmeyer and hugged her too, thanking her for not only taking care of Bethany and me, but also driving us all the way out into the "boonies." Mrs. Cragmeyer went rigid.

I stood beside my sister. "Amelie is happy to see us," I whispered.

Bethany shoved her sketchbook into her Juicy hobo bag, removed her cell phone, and began texting.

Okay, so the talking thing was just a momentary lapse. I'll try to remember that.

I wondered if she was texting her crush Zane, the most popular guy in her grade back home (despite being a class-A jerk). I knew better than to ask. She'd been crushing on Zane for as long as I could remember, and he never noticed her until after our parents died. I guess being an orphan made Bethany more interesting to him. One time I'd tried telling Bethany that Zane isn't a good guy, but that had been a mistake—a serious mistake.

Amelie thanked Mr. Cragmeyer through the open car window. I knew he'd never leave the safety of the car—he feared getting pulverized by one of Amelie's monster hugs.

Mrs. Cragmeyer sniffed. "Amelie, I must ask you to calm down."

"Sure, Linda." Amelie replied, but her crazy grin remained plastered on her face.

Mrs. Cragmeyer glowered like a cartoon bulldog when Amelie called her by her first name. I didn't even know Mrs. Cragmeyer *had* a first name.

Beside me, Bethany's cell phone beeped with a new text message. My sister read the text and frowned. She dropped her cell phone back into her bag. "Stop looking at me," she hissed.

I skirted my sister, opened the trunk of the Olds, and began removing our luggage. Yet the whole time, I kept my eyes on Mrs. Cragmeyer and Amelie. Amelie smiled at the older woman. "Are you sure you don't want to spend the night? It's a long drive back."

"No, thank you. We should be going. My daughter lives in Canton, so we'll stop there on the way home."

"How about a quick lunch? Or just coffee?"

Mrs. Cragmeyer shook her head. "Your offer is very kind, but we must be going. We want to get to our daughter's by dinnertime."

"All right then," Amelie said. "Thank you for everything. It was so generous of you to care for the girls so they didn't have to change schools before the end of the year."

Mrs. Cragmeyer smiled, and her chest inflated with pride. "It was no trouble. It was the Christian thing to do."

Amelie nodded and pulled our backpacks from the backseat of the Olds.

Mrs. Cragmeyer rounded the back of the car, put her arms around Bethany's and my shoulders, and gave the two of us a squeeze. "Now girls, remember what I told you. You have my phone number. Call me *any* time, and Mr. Cragmeyer and I will come fetch you."

I gave her a weak smile in response, but I suspected that I'd be losing Mrs. Cragmeyer's telephone number pretty quickly. Bethany nodded. She was probably wondering how she could see the friends she'd left behind, rather than thinking about the Cragmeyers.

After giving us one final squeeze, the older woman turned back to my aunt. "Now, Amelie, if you find that you can't ..." She paused and then tried again. "If it becomes too taxing for you to care for the girls, remember that Mr. Cragmeyer and I would love to have them with us."

Amelie's eyes narrowed. "That's kind of you to offer. But my brother left their care in my hands, and I plan to fulfill his wishes."

"If you need anything, girls, you know where to reach us," the older woman said loud enough for everyone to hear. Mr. Cragmeyer started up the Olds, and his wife climbed into the front seat of the car. As they backed out of the drive, Mrs. Cragmeyer just shook her head and pinched her lips tight.

I glanced at the house next door and noticed a boy and an older woman staring at us. Although she was probably the same age as Mrs. Cragmeyer, this woman didn't look anything like my former guardian. Her white hair was secured in two stubby pigtails, and she wore a hot pink T-shirt and yellow capris. The boy looked about my age. He wore glasses and had brown hair that fell over the top of his frames.

The woman waved. I waved back. She called out in a clear voice, "Hey, Amelie! Are these your nieces?"

Amelie set down our suitcases. "Come on, girls. I want you to meet some people."

Bethany and I followed her across the yard.

"Hi, Bergita," Amelie said. As we climbed the porch steps behind her, Amelie wrapped an arm around each of our shoulders. "This is Bethany; she'll start eighth grade in the fall. And this is Andi; she'll be in sixth grade."

Bergita grinned, showing off her straight white teeth. "Bergita Carter. Pleased to meet you. And welcome to the neighborhood! I heard what happened to your parents, and I'm really sorry. I knew your father when he was a little boy. Smart as a whip. I always knew Killdeer was too small for him."

Bethany pulled away from Amelie and reached for her cell phone again. I stared at my feet. I never knew what to say when my parents were mentioned.

"This is my grandson, Colin."

I looked up.

Colin pushed his glasses up on the bridge of his nose, smiling shyly. "Hi."

Bethany looked Colin up and down and then sighed as she returned her attention to her phone.

Bergita pointed to a pug lying on a pillow by the front door. "That lazy bum is Jackson."

The dog opened his eyes when he heard his name and snorted into his pillow.

Bethany's head snapped up. "Did that dog just snort?"

"Yes," Colin said. "Pugs are a brachycephalic breed, which means they have a broad head and a short nose. This can cause snorting or sometimes respiratory problems. But don't worry; Jackson is healthy. We take good care of him."

Bethany rolled her eyes.

"If you see two harried-looking doctor types around here, they are my son and daughter-in-law. Then again, you might not see them. They're never home."

Colin grimaced.

Bergita fixed her snappy dark eyes on me. "It's hard to believe that your parents would name their first girl Bethany and their second girl Andi."

I grinned. "My name is actually Andora, but I go by Andi most of the time."

Bergita took a quick breath. "Andora?"

Concerned, Amelie put a hand on Bergita's arm. "Bergita, what is it?"

A strange look crossed Bergita's face. Then the expression was quickly gone. Bergita laughed, "Oh, it's nothing. I must have had some bad egg salad for lunch. Won't do that again! Come along, Colin. Let's leave the girls to get settled in."

I glanced behind me as I followed my aunt and sister across Bergita's yard. The older woman was still watching me with an odd look on her face.

"Welcome home!" Amelie announced as we stepped through the front door. The house looked just as I remembered it. When we were younger, my parents used to bring Bethany and me to our grandparents' house for quick visits around Christmas, Easter, or the Fourth of July. But I hadn't been to the house since I was seven—after my grandmother died. And then my dad and aunt had boarded up the house because they didn't know what else to do with it. They couldn't sell it because it had been in the family for so long. Yet at the same time, neither one of them expected to ever live there again.

The house was too far away from my parents' work at Cleveland State University, and my aunt never stayed in one place for very long. She'd hopped from country to country on her quest to see the world. At least, she hadn't *planned* to stay in one place until she got a job as an English professor at Michael Pike University. But now she was stuck with two kids. I worried my lip. Were Bethany and I holding Amelie back from her life?

A ginger-colored cat wove in and around my sister's legs. The tiniest of smiles played on Bethany's lips. Then the cat did the same thing to me. We'd always wanted a pet, but our parents said no because they traveled so much.

"Well, Mr. Rochester," Amelie said with a laugh. "The girls have arrived, and I see you've given them the proper greeting."

He meowed loudly in response.

"Can I pick him up?" Bethany asked. It was the first thing she'd said to our aunt since we'd arrived.

Amelie's face broke into a smile. "Of course! He's a very friendly gentleman."

Bethany slipped her phone into the pocket of her jeans and picked up Mr. Rochester. The orange cat settled into her arms, and Bethany left the room.

Amelie's mouth twisted as she watched her niece go.

Later that night, I stood on top of a bed in the room that I would now share with my sister. I was hanging my favorite poster of the periodic table on the wall.

Bethany sat on the floor folding her countless pairs of Lucky jeans and Abercrombie tops. "I don't want that poster hanging up in here."

I froze with a piece of turquoise Sticky Tack hanging from my pointer finger. "Why not?"

"It makes me feel like I'm in school. I don't need to be reminded of school when I'm in my room. And you don't have to show off all of your science geek stuff anymore. There's no one here to impress with it."

I flinched. She was referring to our parents, of course. I knew she was. I smoothed the poster on the wall and said, "It's my room too."

Bethany slammed the bottom dresser drawer. Mr. Rochester, who'd been lying on the end of my bed, jumped and ran out of the room. It was half the size of either Bethany's or my bedroom in the house we'd shared with our parents. "And don't think you're getting even one drawer in this chest," she warned me.

As I sat on the bed, I felt a hard knot tighten in the pit of my stomach. I lay down and stretched out on my side. "It's not my fault we're here."

When I didn't say anything more, Bethany slammed the drawer shut a second time and flopped onto her own bed. The beds had matching blue plaid comforters and cotton blue sheets covered with thousands of tiny yellow daisies. The sheets still had the creases in them from the packaging.

Bethany turned over on her side and glared at me. "Let's get this straight right now: This is my room, and I'm *letting* you sleep here. Don't touch anything."

I stared at the ceiling. Someone had painted it the

same bright blue as the ocean in my parents' photographs of Belize. *What happened to those photographs?* I wondered. I felt Bethany's glare. She knew what I was thinking. "Don't talk about them. Don't say anything about them. Understand? We're starting over here, and it's better if we forget."

I squeezed my eyes shut to hold back the tears.

In a rare moment of softness, Bethany whispered, "It will be too hard on us if we don't."

I rolled over and faced the wall.

The next morning I awoke to the sound of faint, anxious murmurs floating up the stairs. And once I'm awake, I can never fall back asleep. The murmurs didn't seem to bother Bethany who continued snoring softly on her side of our deeply divided bedroom. After stretching my arms and crawling out of bed, I pulled on a sweatshirt over my pajamas and followed the whispers down the hall.

I crept halfway down the stairs and crouched on the fifth step. In her tie-dye pajama bottoms and strawberry pink sweatshirt, Amelie looked more like one of my classmates than a college professor. Through the wooden railing, I could see she was perched on the living room sofa with her knees tucked close to her chest, talking on the phone. "I know you've been waiting for this a long time. So have I … but I told you, there's no way I can go …"

Mr. Rochester, who was lounging on the back of the couch like a lazy sea lion sunning itself on the shoreline, blinked at me. Then he jumped to the floor and pranced up the steps to sit beside me.

"I wish you would understand …" Amelie said to the person on the other end of the line. "It's not like I planned for my brother to die in a plane crash …" She paused and said more quietly, "You're right. That wasn't fair …"

I wondered who Amelie was speaking to and what that person had said to upset her. *And what did any of this have to do with Dad?* I wondered. What did it have to do with my sister and me? Were we holding Amelie back from living her big exciting life like I'd feared? What kid wanted to be a burden?

"I want to stay here with the girls. I need to be here with them. We need each other … I'm sorry you can't understand that … But I'm sure you can find someone else to go with you … Oh … you already have?" A tear slid down her sun-kissed cheek. "That's probably for the best. Well, I have to go now. The girls will be up soon."

She turned off the cordless phone and looked dazed for a minute. I fidgeted on the carpeted step, and my leg slid to a more comfortable position. Amelie glanced up.

"Andi!" she yelped. "How long have you been sitting there?"

I swallowed. "Not long. Sorry."

Her eyes still watery, she smiled at me.

I couldn't help myself and asked, "Who were you talking to?"

She looked down at the phone. "Not long, huh?" Then she met my inquisitive stare with a knowing grin. "It was just a friend."

I walked down the stairs and flopped down beside her on the couch. "Did you have to cancel a trip because of us?"

She gave my shoulder a squeeze. "Well, aren't you nosey?"

I shrugged, nonchalant. "That's what Bethany says."

In our old house, Bethany would set her easel by the huge windows in the great room. She said it had good morning light. I don't know how many times I sneaked into the room and tried to see her paintings before they were done. Every time she caught me, and every time she'd say, "Well, aren't you nosey, Andi?" But eventually she would show me the painting. I didn't think she would show me one of her paintings now.

Amelie said, "I guess it comes with the territory. I was a pretty nosey kid when I was your age." She leaned in closer and chuckled. "I think it's a little sister thing. But to answer your question, I was going to travel to England this summer for a research trip. My colleague was upset that I have to back out."

I stared at my orange socks. "Because of Bethany and me."

She bumped my shoulder with hers. "Sometimes it's hard for people to understand that now and again family has to come first. That's what I was trying to tell this person on the phone. I can go to England another time. It's not going anywhere."

"Are you sure this person is just a colleague?"

She laughed. "Did you sleep well?" She lowered her body onto the yoga mat on the floor and began stretching her long legs.

I shrugged. Every hour or so, I'd woken up to hear Bethany's snoring or the old house groaning as it settled deeper into the earth. Sometimes both.

"I'm glad," she said, jumping to her feet. "Would you like some breakfast?"

I followed her into the kitchen, a room filled with windows that were now dimmed by the dark, brooding skies outside. I stared out one of the windows as Amelie floated about the room like a colorful bird. The sky looked like what I'd expect to see on the day of a funeral. Although, on the day we buried my parents, it had been unseasonably warm and the sun shone in a periwinkle sky. Today's sky would have worked better for me then; it was a sky that let me stay angry.

Amelie peered out the window, "Looks like it's going to be a doozy." She turned on the frosted glass ceiling light. As if she'd beckoned it by flipping on the electrical switch, the trees outside the kitchen windows bent almost in half from a wind gust that indicated the coming storm. The clouds churned to life. But no water splashed against the windows. The ground outside appeared dry, and the clouds swelled with the heavy burden they refused to release. The rain, it seemed, was holding back for the perfect moment. I wondered if it was waiting for a funeral to begin. I hoped not.

Amelie opened a cupboard and peered inside. "The weather is supposed to be bad all day. Kind of a crummy way to start the summer, don't you think? But it should clear off by tomorrow."

I nodded and climbed onto a tall stool by the breakfast bar.

"Are Honey Nut Cheerios okay? I used to like them when I was a kid, and I didn't know what you guys like to eat for breakfast."

"Cheerios are great," I said. Hands-down, they would beat the runny eggs that Mrs. Cragmeyer insisted I eat every morning for the last few weeks. I'd be happy if I never ate another egg as long as I lived.

Amelie pulled the cereal box out of the cupboard and placed it, a bowl and a spoon, and a half-gallon of milk in front of me on the breakfast bar.

"Did you already have breakfast?" I asked.

She shook her head and grabbed a second bowl and spoon for herself. She ate her cereal while standing at the counter. After we'd settled into our breakfast, Amelie said, "You know, Andi, I really am glad that you and Bethany are here. I know we haven't spent that much time together. And that's my fault. I should have made more of an effort. But now I'm looking forward to getting to know both of you a lot better. Despite our disagreements, I loved your dad and mom very much. And I love you and Bethany just as much."

I took a big bite of Cheerios.

As if she sensed my discomfort, Amelie asked, "Is there anything you want to ask me?"

I asked the first question that popped into my head

that wasn't about my parents. "Why do you think Bergita acted so weird when I told her my full name yesterday?"

The neighbor lady's peculiar reaction had bounced around in my mind all night while I listened to the house murmur in the darkness. It was easier to wonder about that than the other questions that plagued my thoughts. Like why my parents died in that plane crash in Guatemala.

She grinned. "You sure are inquisitive. Your dad told me you want to be a scientist like him and Paula. You're on the right track with such acute observation skills."

I grinned. "Do you know?"

"You're persistent too. Always a good trait in a scientist." She shrugged. "Who knows why Bergita does anything? You can't take what she says or does too seriously. You'll learn that as you get to know her better."

I wrinkled my nose. I may not know Bergita, but there was more to it than that.

"Maybe it *was* the egg salad," Amelie added with a laugh. "I've had Bergita's egg salad before. Horrible stuff. She has an affection for mayonnaise that's just wrong. If she offers it to you, I suggest you run the other way. She's a wonderful baker though. Her blueberry muffins are phenomenal." She ate a big spoonful of Cheerios, and I realized that she'd finished her last bite before I'd spooned my second one. "Any other burning questions?"

I hesitated before asking, "Can I have my own room?"

Amelie thought for a minute. "You guys aren't getting along?"

I shrugged and concentrated on sinking Cheerios with my spoon. The sunken Os bobbed back to the surface, creating tiny milk waves.

Amelie nodded as if she understood. "Well, let me make you a deal."

"Okay," I said, sitting up. I'd do anything to have my own room.

"I've been meaning to clean out the attic for a long time. Nothing's been done with it since Mom died. I just shove more and more junk up there and close the hatch before it can fall and crush me to death. But when we were kids, the attic was your dad's bedroom. If you clean it out and organize it, it can be your room."

"Really?" I dropped my spoon into the bowl, sending honey-flavored Cheerios sailing to the bowl's ceramic sides.

"Our neighborhood has a massive garage sale every summer. Bergita is the organizer, so it's not your typical sale. She pulls out all the stops. If you finish the project by then, we can sell most of the stuff there." She placed her bowl and spoon in the dishwasher. "It's in a couple of weeks. I don't usually participate in the garage sale because it's the same weekend as the Endless Summer Festival, an arts and activity fair at the university. But with you and Bethany helping, I bet we could pull it off. And then you and your sister can split the profits."

I wiggled happily on the barstool. For a minute, I fantasized about having my own room and enough money to buy a new microscope. "When can I start?"

Amelie glanced out the window. "I was going to take you girls to the park today to show you my old haunts. But with this weather ... today is as good a day as any."

I jumped off the stool. "Let's go look at it now."

She gave me a huge smile. "Why not?"

We raced up the stairs and then tiptoed past the room I shared with Bethany, giggling when we heard a loud snore from behind the closed door. It reminded me of when Bethany and I would tiptoe around our house after our parents got home from a long research expedition. They were always so tired. We knew we'd be in trouble if we woke them, but we couldn't help but laugh every time we crept by their door.

We walked past Amelie's bedroom, the only full bathroom in the house, and a linen closet before coming to the end of the upstairs hallway. Amelie yanked hard on a white rope dangling from the ceiling. As she pulled open the attic hatch, a folded ladder appeared. And then a cloud of dust tumbled through the opening. Amelie sneezed. "I haven't been up there in a while."

I stepped out of the way as she unfolded the ladder.

"I'll let you go first," she said.

Slowly, I climbed the ladder as the rungs groaned under my weight.

"Be careful," Amelie warned.

A beam of light fought its way through the dark stormy sky, the grimy windowpane, and a mountain of clutter as I made my way to the top of the creaky ladder. There were boxes everywhere—wooden boxes, cardboard boxes, plastic boxes, and metal boxes. I suspected that the lump in the far corner of the room was Dad's old bed.

Amelie poked her head up through the hatch like a meerkat on the African savannah. She sneezed again. "This place is a mess. Are you sure you want to tackle it?"

I looked around the room at the dusty boxes, sheet-covered furniture, and the cobwebby corners. And I truly smiled for the first time in months. "Yeah, I really do."

"Andi! Lunchtime!" Amelie's voice floated up through the hatch.

"Just a minute!" I called back. I flipped through my grandparents' wedding album. They looked so happy together. Grandma wore a simple white dress, and Grandpa wore a dark suit. The pair in the photo stood in front of Amelie's big yellow house on Dunlap Avenue. I guess it's my house now, too. The grainy images of my grandfather caught my attention. He looked so much like my dad. My eyes stung. Father and son had the same wide smile, big ears, and laughing eyes.

The attic was hot and stuffy, and when I blinked it seemed like more junk miraculously appeared. I sighed. The project was bigger than I first thought. No wonder Amelie hadn't bothered with it, not that I could imagine my hyperactive aunt sitting anywhere for more than five minutes unless she was twisted into a yoga pose. I'd been upstairs for three hours and hadn't made a dent.

I closed the album and set it on top of a box. Boxes and furniture surrounded me on all sides. I hadn't accomplished much in the way of sorting since Amelie had left me in the attic that morning. But I did manage to wade through the room and clear off a place to sit on the wooden floor.

I stood and dusted myself off. A clap of thunder shook the house and startled me so bad that I tripped over a stack of books and tumbled into a soft pile of old tablecloths. After getting back on my feet and weaving my way through more stacks of junk, I started down the ladder.

When I walked into the kitchen, I saw Bethany sitting hunched over the breakfast bar and eating a turkey sandwich.

"Is turkey okay, Andi?" Amelie piled turkey on a slice of wheat bread.

I nodded.

Amelie slid a plate in front of me. "Do you still draw, Bethany?"

"Yeah," she answered. But her tone said, *So what?* She picked the crust off her sandwich and stared at her plate.

Amelie forced a cheerful smile. "Bergita—the lady next door—likes to paint and draw too. I told her about you and all of the beautiful pieces you've made for me over the years. She's taking a painting class at the university this summer. It's not too late to register.

And since I'm on the faculty there, I'm sure I can get you a spot in the class."

"Maybe," Bethany said as she picked up her phone and looked at it. She frowned. "My phone's not working."

Amelie snapped her fingers. "That's because I got you a new one so you could be on my cell phone plan. Your old one has been deactivated."

Bethany's mouth fell open. "Deactivated?"

This wasn't going to go well.

Amelie opened a drawer and removed a blue cell phone that was almost identical to my sister's. "It's the same phone number. Some of the features are different though."

Bethany's eyes narrowed. "What features?"

"I had to change your plan to save money, so no more unlimited texting. Between us, we have just one hundred texts a month."

"What? I send that many texts in a day."

"You will have to be more careful then."

Bethany blinked. I knew she was trying not to cry. "Why do you need to save money? What about all the money you got from Mom and Dad? I know there is money."

My aunt stepped back and bumped into the corner of the open dishwasher door. "That money was put into a trust fund for your college education. I can't use it to pay your cell phone bill."

"If I can't text, then how am I going to talk to anyone?"

"If you want the texting plan, you can pay for it yourself. Andi started cleaning out the attic so she can move in up there. If you help her, you two can split the profits from the garage sale."

"That won't be enough to pay my cell phone bill forever."

"No, but it's a start," Amelie said and then paused. "And you can always look for a part-time job. Baby-sitting or something like that."

"Baby-sitting? You want me to *baby-sit*?" Bethany grabbed both cell phones and stormed out of the kitchen.

Amelie sighed. "I messed up the phone thing, didn't I?"

I gave her a half smile and bit into my sandwich.

I was helping Amelie clean up the kitchen when the doorbell rang.

Amelie started clearing the table. "Would you get that, Andi?"

I ran to the front door. When I opened it, I found Colin standing on the doorstep holding a bright orange umbrella. "Hi." He pushed his bangs off his glasses, and I noticed his eyes were the same color as his hair, somewhere between hot cocoa and dark chocolate.

"Hi," I replied.

He closed his umbrella and tapped it nervously against his leg, unaware of the wet spot it made on his shorts.

Amelie stepped into the living room. "Colin, don't just stand out there in the rain. Come in! Would you like some lunch?"

Colin left his umbrella on the porch and stepped into the house. "We just ate."

I perched on the edge of the sofa, itching to go back to the attic.

Colin shifted from foot to foot and stared at his shoes.

Amelie cocked her head. "Well, do you want to help Andi with a special project?"

My head snapped up, and I gaped at my aunt.

Colin grinned, obviously relieved. "What is it?"

"She's cleaning out the attic so she can turn it into her bedroom. You still interested?"

"Sure. I bet there's a bunch of cool old stuff up there."

Amelie glanced at me. "Would it be okay if Colin helped you?"

Did I have a choice? I put my hands in my pockets. "If he wants to, but I haven't found anything that exciting."

She grinned. "You will. You guys go ahead, and I'll be up in a little while."

Back in the stuffy attic, I wedged myself into my nest on the hardwood floor, and Colin sat down on an old trunk.

"What do you want me to do?" he asked.

I spun around to get a better view of him. His hair clung to his damp forehead. It was twenty degrees warmer in the attic than in the rest of the house.

"The first thing we can do is move the boxes and furniture around so we both have plenty of space to work," I said.

"Sounds like a plan." Colin agreed. "Look at all this stuff. And I thought *our* attic was bad."

"Amelie hasn't had time to do anything with the attic since my grandparents died."

Colin held up his hand. "There must be decades of stuff up here. Put me to work."

I studied him to make sure he was serious, and his expression looked genuine. "Just pick a spot and start clearing. The trash bags are over there."

A loud clap of thunder shook the attic. Colin yelped and jumped three feet into the air.

I laughed.

He said, "I hope Bergita is sitting with Jackson. He's afraid of thunderstorms."

"You call your grandma 'Bergita'?"

He shrugged and adjusted his glasses. "She's more like a 'Bergita' than a 'Grandma.'"

Thunder clapped again. "The storm is only a few miles away," Colin said.

"This is nothing compared to the storms my dad saw in Central America. He always said the lightning there could skin a cat ..." My voice trailed off. I'd learned over the last few weeks that most kids don't like to hear about someone's dead parents. They don't like to be reminded that it could happen to them too.

Mr. Rochester, who'd been lounging beside me on a pile of old newspapers, meowed as if offended by my skinned-cat comment.

"Sorry, Mr. Rochester. No one would ever think of doing that to you." I scratched behind his left ear.

Colin started moving boxes from a spot close to the window. "Amelie said they went to Guatemala a lot."

I opened a box that was full to bursting with dusty artificial flowers, and I sneezed. "Yeah, they did. They were working with some other scientists down there, looking for endangered plants."

After a bout of coughs and sneezes, Colin said, "I'm sorry about your parents."

"Thanks."

I rearranged a group of boxes so I could sit closer to the wall and lean against it while I sorted through the flowers. *If I could somehow remove the years of dust from these silk petals and leaves,* I thought, *they might make good sellers at the garage sale.* After we moved the boxes, I noticed the lower half of the wall was wallpapered from the floor up to my hip. Red and blue sailboats rocked on a gentle sea. The once-white billows of the ships were now yellowed like pages of really old books.

I stared at the wallpaper, thinking about my father as a little boy choosing that particular pattern because boats are symbols of adventure, of moving, of being somewhere else. My father always wanted to be somewhere else. Even after Bethany and I were born, he and my mother never stayed home much. Too many endangered plants in the forests of the world needed to be saved. The forests were too remote for us to join our globetrotting parents. During those times, just like we'd done during the last few weeks since the funeral, we'd stayed with the Cragmeyers.

A bright flash of lightning bounced off a piece of metal on the far wall. But when I looked more closely, the glint of metal disappeared. I crawled on my hands and knees to the spot.

"What is it?" Colin asked.

"I thought I saw something." I pointed at the area where I'd seen the reflection.

"A ghost?" Colin asked. His eyes were the size of ping-pong balls.

"No, not a ghost. A piece of metal."

"What's so interesting about that?"

"I only saw it when the lightning flashed." I tapped the wall. "It was right around here."

Colin wove his way through the maze of boxes and squatted down beside me, forcing me to scoot over until my hip thwacked into the corner of an old maple dresser. Colin ran his hand up and down over the wallpaper. Abruptly, his palm froze while his fingers continued to tickle a particular spot in the wallpaper. "There's something here."

"Move your hand," I said.

He did, and I put my own palm in its place. "What is it?" I asked.

"It felt like a hinge."

"Like a door hinge?"

"Yeah."

We looked at each other.

Colin asked, "Do you think we should open it?"

I slid my fingernail under the edge of the old paper. With a good grip, I peeled away a wide strip. Colin joined in. Piece by piece, the red and blue sailboats fell to the floor in shreds. The old glue, which had held the wallpaper onto the wall for all those years, posed no match for us. Sections of wallpaper came off in larger and larger pieces, leaving whole sailboats intact.

Finally, the scraps of discarded wallpaper revealed an outline of a small door in the wall. It looked nearly two feet high with no doorknob. The hinges made only the slightest bump on the wall, about the length of my thumb. Someone had drilled a small hole where a tiny doorknob should have been. I fit my pinkie finger into it. "How do we get in?" I asked.

Colin stood up and pieces of wallpaper floated to the floor. "There has to be something up here we could use. A screwdriver or a hammer, maybe?" He began opening boxes, and I joined in. Dust flew through the air as we rifled past generations of clutter. Colin sneezed but paused only a moment to wipe his nose on his dust-covered sleeve before continuing to look for the right tool.

"What about this?" I asked. I held up a silver letter opener with a tiger engraved on the handle.

"That should work."

We knelt outside the door again. I slid the letter opener between the wall and the door. Colin spat on the hinges, and a few specks of his saliva hit my face.

"What are you doing?" I asked, wiping his spit from my eye.

"These hinges are old. I'm trying to lubricate them so the door opens easier. I saw it in a movie once."

"Oh, good idea. Kinda gross, but still a good idea."

He spat a couple more times, and I bent the letter opener against the wall, pressing down hard.

Snap! The tip of the letter opener broke off and clattered to the floor on the other side of the door. Luckily, the pressure from the blade cracked the door just enough so I could get my fingers around the edge. Colin did the same. "On the count of three," I said.

We counted together. "One ... two ... three!" And then we pulled with all our might. Colin huffed with exertion beside me, and his face turned beet red.

The old hinges finally relented, and Colin and I toppled to the floor. I landed on his stomach—hard. A cloud of blue-black dust flew out of the open door like confetti. We both scrambled to our feet, waving the dust from our faces, coughing and gagging as we inhaled the musty scent of the long-forgotten crawlspace.

"Do you see anything?"

"Nothing." Colin sneezed as the last bit of dust settled onto the floor.

I reached my hand into the black hole. My hand ran into something hard and square. "I think it's a trunk! Help me pull it out."

Colin squeezed beside me, and together we pulled out the trunk. It was about twice the size of a shoebox, and it looked as if it were meant to hold a doll's clothes. Blue cracked leather covered the lid and peeled away from the trunk's brass edges. I ran my hand over the uneven top. Colin scooted up beside me and peered closer at the old lock. He wiped the grime away with his T-shirt.

"Look," he said.

I turned my gaze to where he was pointing and saw one word engraved on the trunk's brass nameplate: ANDORA.

"I hope you guys like Kool-Aid," Amelie announced, her head peeking through the open hatch. "What happened in here?" She climbed the rest of the way into the attic and put the drink bottles on top of an old dresser. "What on earth?"

Colin's face turned an astonishing shade of red.

I jumped up. "I can explain." I waded through the clutter toward my aunt and grabbed her hand. "Look what we found!" I led her back over to the corner. "There was a door hidden behind the wallpaper. And look! There was a trunk inside."

Amelie grinned. "What's in the trunk?"

"We don't know yet," Colin said, his color fading back to normal. "We haven't opened it."

Amelie squatted down and looked at the lock and the name etched in brass. "Andora," she whispered.

She stared at me in amazement, and I shrugged. "Colin, there's a black crowbar hanging on the far wall of the garage that should do the job. Will you go get it, please?"

After Colin clattered down the ladder, Amelie said, "Well, we know one thing."

"What?" I asked. I stared at the trunk trying to guess what was inside. Gold? Rubies? Diamonds? Valuable old baseball cards? Or just old clothes?

"Whatever is in that box is yours," Amelie said.

"But ..."

Amelie ran her hand over the trunk and grinned at me, "Hey, your name's on it."

I grinned back. "You're right. It is."

A moment later Colin's head appeared through the hatch. Out of breath, he handed the crowbar to Amelie, who then handed it to me. "You do the honors, Andi."

I placed the flat tip between the lock and the trunk lid and pressed down with all of my weight. The lock was stubborn and held for a few seconds until—*crack!*— it swung from its hinge and crashed to the floor.

We squatted in front of the tiny trunk again. Using the crowbar to pry it open, I lifted the lid. A thin layer of tissue paper covered the contents. I gently picked up the paper and set it on another box nearby. The tissue crackled like dry leaves. Beneath the paper was a doll—a lovely, fragile china doll like those I'd seen in old Shirley Temple movies. The doll's face was snow white with bright red lips. Her cheeks were perfectly round pink circles just below her large blue eyes. She wore a faded dress the color of summer cornflowers. I picked up the doll and handed it to Amelie.

"She's beautiful," Amelie said.

Colin wasn't impressed with the doll and peered past it into the trunk. "What else is in there?" I think he hoped the little blue trunk contained a hoard of gold coins or rubies. Maybe I hoped the same.

The doll had been lying on some folded pieces of fabric. I unfolded each one and found two dresses—for a toddler maybe—and a white dress for an infant. One of the little girl's dresses was pink. The other was pale yellow. Both were covered in ruffles. Amelie said the infant's dress looked like a baptismal gown. Yellowed like the sailboats' paper sails, the gown had a matching bonnet covered with tiny pearls.

At the very bottom of the trunk, we found three wooden blocks labeled A, B, and C with circus clowns and animals painted on the other sides. A clown put his head into a lion's mouth; an elephant balanced on his hind legs on top of a beach ball; and six tiny clowns stuffed themselves into an even tinier car.

"What is all this?" I asked after we'd sorted through each piece. "How old do you think this stuff is?"

Amelie looked at the dresses and wooden blocks. "Probably mid-twentieth century, I would guess. Maybe around World War Two, possibly earlier."

That got Colin's attention. "Cool!"

It must have been the war part.

Amelie held the baptismal bonnet in her hand and gave it to me before standing up. "Looks like you have a mystery on your hands."

At dinnertime, I asked Amelie again, "Are you sure you don't know who Andora is?"

She popped a tater tot into her mouth and said, "When your dad told me he named you Andora, it was the first time I'd heard that name. It's pretty unusual. I think I would've recognized it if I'd heard it before."

"But don't you think it's weird that there's a trunk in the attic with my name on it?"

Bethany pulverized her tater tots, smashing them into barely recognizable potato shreds. "Andi, you've been talking about it *all day*. What does it matter? If that stuff is really that old, then Andora is probably dead by now."

I dropped my eyes to the boxed macaroni and cheese on my plate.

"That's not necessarily true, Bethany. The person would be very old, in her eighties or nineties, but she could still be alive," Amelie said.

I let out a breath. "Maybe you can help Colin and me tomorrow. I bet you'll find stuff to use for your art projects."

Bethany hopped off her stool. "I'm going upstairs to send my *one* text message for the day."

"Okay," Amelie said.

Whenever Bethany used that snippy tone with our parents, they grounded her on the spot. But life with Amelie was different, and maybe it was just what Bethany needed.

That night, I crept out of my bedroom and climbed the ladder into the attic. With a weak flashlight beam to guide me, I picked my way through the decades of castoff, forgotten keepsakes until I was back by the hidden door and the little blue trunk. I opened it again and examined each piece slowly. No answers jumped out at me, but in the dim glow of my flashlight, the trunk seemed so much more mysterious. I had to find out where it came from.

I held the wooden block with the elephant painted on it. I turned it over and over again in my hand until the images blurred. Tomorrow, I would find out who this other Andora was and why her life was hidden away in a little blue trunk.

The next morning, I stepped onto the porch a little after seven. No one else was up yet. Just like Dad used to do, I always wake up with the sun. He told me dawn was the best time of the day in Guatemala City, when the city shook itself awake. He promised he would take me there someday.

"You're up early!" A voice interrupted my thoughts.

I spun to the left and saw Bergita with a mug in her hand. She was pitching back and forth on one of the cane rocking chairs on her front porch. Jackson snoozed on his pillow by the front door.

I skipped down the porch steps and trotted across the lawn. I paused at the foot of Bergita's porch steps.

"This is certainly a pleasant surprise. I like to see young people up bright and early, ready to tackle the new day. Have a seat." She motioned to the opposite rocker. On the small table between us, a perspiring teapot and a second mug waited as if they'd been expecting me. Also sitting on the table was a small plate holding two lumpy pastries I didn't recognize.

Before sitting down, I patted Jackson on the head. The snub-nosed dog opened one brown eye, closed it, and made a happy snuffle sound.

Bergita set down her Daffy Duck mug and poured some tea into a faded mug with Bugs Bunny wagging a carrot on it.

She held the plate of pastries out toward me, and I took one, realizing for the first time how hungry I was. The night before, I'd barely eaten a thing because I'd been so excited about the mysterious Andora.

"What are these?" I asked, taking a small bite. It tasted both salty and sweet, and it had the consistency of an extra thick biscuit.

Crumbs fell onto my lap, and Jackson was up in a flash, sitting beside me with an I'm-starving-to-death look on his face. I brushed the crumbs off my T-shirt and shorts. He licked them off the floorboards.

"These," Bergita held up her own pastry, "are called scones. They are an English pastry, and I just love them. I've eaten one every day for the last forty years, so they must be good for something."

I took a bigger bite. When Bergita wasn't looking, I broke off a small piece and slipped it to Jackson. He ate it and snuffled my palm with his nose. Now friends for life, the dog lay across my feet and went to sleep. He was surprisingly heavy.

Bergita licked her index finger to pick up the

crumbs off her plate. "The perfect start to any day," she declared. "Colin enjoyed himself yesterday."

I stiffened, wondering if Colin had told his grandmother about our discovery. It was my story to tell. After all, my name was on the trunk. "I'm glad," I said, before sipping my tea. I held the mug in both hands— just like Bergita. One hand grasped the handle; the other cupped the bottom rim. "What did Colin say?"

She grinned and resumed rocking back and forth, "Not much. Just that he helped you clean up the attic. Colin's a funny kid like that. Perhaps he enjoyed the company more than the activity." She winked at me.

A blush much hotter than the tea crept up my cheeks and into my pink hairline. I gritted my teeth.

I stumbled over the use of her first name, but somehow "Mrs. Carter" didn't seem right. "Bergita?"

"Yes?" Bergita rocked gently in her chair. She sipped her tea while looking out over her lawn and flower gardens.

I gnawed the inside of my cheek, wondering if I should ask the question that nagged me. But my mother had said the most important characteristic of a scientist was not being afraid to ask uncomfortable questions. I figured if I wanted to be a scientist like my parents someday, I'd better get used to asking the tough questions now. "Did you know someone else named Andora?"

She didn't seem surprised by the question. She rocked and sipped, and rocked and sipped. I shifted in my chair, waiting, holding back the dozens of other questions that were now bouncing around inside my head. *A scientist must also be patient and wait for the results*, I told myself. Scone and impatience gurgled together in my belly. I sipped the tea carefully, hoping to settle my stomach.

Bergita placed a hand on her chin. "I *have* heard your name before. Long, long ago when I was just a child." She smacked her lips in thought. "I was seven years old during the summer of 1946, and I was excited about starting the second grade because I'd have my own Aunt Maribeth for my teacher. One afternoon, I attended a church picnic and ran around with the boys, as usual." She wrinkled her nose. "I was a real Dickens back then."

"Dickens?"

She smiled. "A trouble-making child similar to the street urchins in Charles Dickens' novels. The boys and I tried to snatch extra cookies from the picnic table. I knew my mother didn't want me to have any more.

"Anyway, two women were standing at the table: Mrs. Frieda Baptist and Mrs. Louanne Mayes. Both of them are gone now, of course, but I overheard their conversation. Mrs. Baptist said, 'Poor man. Nothing seems to hold him together.' And then Mrs. Mayes said, 'He still has the boy.'

"I wondered who they were talking about, and I snuck closer because I knew they were talking about someone at the picnic. I loved overhearing all of the scuttlebutt around church and then reporting back to Grandma Daisy. She was too ill to attend services with us.

"Mrs. Baptist said, 'Andora, too,' but then Mrs. Mayes snapped, 'Bite your tongue!' Her tone was so harsh, I jumped and knocked the plate of gingersnaps onto the grass."

Bergita laughed. "Boy, were they furious with me for eavesdropping! And as well they should have been. They threatened to tell my daddy, and I certainly didn't want them to do that. He was a huge bear of a man and had just gotten back from the Pacific. He'd been stationed there during the Second World War. I was glad to have my daddy back, and I didn't want him disappointed with me.

"So I ran home and told my Grandma Daisy what I'd overheard. I just knew she'd eat it up and give me some of her homemade ice cream as a reward. But she didn't have the reaction I'd expected. Usually, she'd grin and rub her hands together, eager for the smallest tidbit of gossip. When I told her this story, however, her lips pursed like she'd taken a big bite of lemon and couldn't spit it out.

"I asked her, 'Who's Andora?' And she snapped at me. I remember it was the first time Grandma Daisy had ever spoken harshly to me in my whole life. 'Shush your mouth, Bergy,' she said. 'I don't want you to ever say that name again. And don't listen to people like Mrs. Baptist who don't have enough sense to leave it alone.'"

"And you never found out which man the two women were talking about?" I asked.

"Never." Bergita took another sip of her tea with a faraway look in her eyes.

The front door to the house opened, and Colin stepped outside. His hair was still wet from a shower, making it appear black. He grinned. "Hi."

"Hi," I replied.

I looked at Bergita and stopped smiling. A smirk played around the corners of her lips. "Andora here was just asking me about her name."

Colin's eyes grew wide as he looked at me. I barely shook my head, hoping he'd guess that I hadn't said anything to Bergita about the hidden trunk. He climbed onto the porch railing, and his bare feet swung back and forth between the smooth maple posts.

"When I met you the other day and I told you my name, you looked ..." I paused, searching for the right word, "... you looked afraid. Why?"

"You have a good eye, my dear." She sighed. "I suppose I was remembering Grandma Daisy's reprimand. Like I said, she'd never yelled at me before. For her to be so upset with me, I knew I should leave it alone. So I never mentioned it again until now." Bergita stood. "I'd better go inside and get my things together for painting class."

"Bethany likes art too. Amelie told her about the class and asked her if she wanted to go." I picked up my mug from the table. "I don't think she will though."

Bergita folded her arms. "She should. It would be a good way for her to meet some other artists in town. Leave it to me. I'll talk your sister into it."

Good luck, I thought but decided to let Bergita come to her own conclusions about Bethany.

The scones long gone, Jackson followed Bergita inside, probably hoping for an after-breakfast snack.

The door latched behind them, and I told Colin the story Bergita had just shared with me.

Colin scratched his chin. It was a gesture that reminded me of someone much older, like Mr. Cragmeyer. "Sounds like there's something about this Andora that the whole town wanted to hide."

"But why?"

Colin jumped off the railing and snapped his fingers. "Let's find out."

I almost dropped my Bugs Bunny mug. "Find out?" I set the mug on the table and brushed the rest of the scone crumbs from my jean shorts.

"You know, investigate." His eyes gleamed, reminding me of Jackson right before I slipped him a piece of scone.

I had to admit that I liked the idea. I'd already planned on doing as much on my own, but maybe I could use Colin's help. He knew more about Killdeer than I did.

"I'll be right back," Colin said, dashing into the house.

I pulled my knees up to my chest and lurched back and forth in the old rocker, thinking about Andora and wondering why my parents named me after someone no one remembered. Had my dad remembered her? I wish I could ask him.

Colin was back within seconds carrying a medium-sized red notebook and an orange pencil with a football eraser on the end. "This is it!" He wrote on the first page, THE CASE OF THE FIRST ANDORA. And under that he added, BOGGS AND CARTER INVESTIGATIONS.

He grinned. "We'll list all of our clues in here and solve the case. First, we need to catalog everything we found in the trunk and where and when we found it. Then we need to copy down Bergita's story."

I dropped my legs to the floor. "We do have one excellent clue so far."

"Yeah, the stuff in the trunk."

"And we know that whoever this Andora was, she was alive before the summer of 1946 when Bergita overheard those ladies gossiping at the picnic."

Colin hopped up and down. "That's right!" He made a note in our new casebook. "I know the perfect place to start looking for more clues."

"Where?"

He slammed the casebook shut. "Do you have a bike?"

We found my red mountain bike sitting in Amelie's garage. I was so glad to have the bicycle back that I didn't care where Colin planned to take me just as long as I could ride there. Mrs. Cragmeyer shipped the bike off to Amelie's house after our house sold because she insisted that I couldn't keep it in the Cragmeyers' garage. She said I'd scratch Mr. Cragmeyer's Oldsmobile.

Colin collected his blue bike from his grandmother's garage, and off we rode. I didn't pay that much attention to where he led me. I was having too much fun letting the wind whip through my pink hair as we pedaled faster and faster. Colin pumped his pedals as fast as he could as we rode through town, past the Victorian and colonial houses, fast-food chains, and the middle school I would attend in the fall.

The brakes of Colin's bike screeched as he skidded to a stop outside the old bottling company. I stopped my bike behind his and dismounted, wishing our bike ride could continue all the way to the equator and back. But I knew there'd be time for bike rides later. Finding this mysterious Andora was more important.

"Now will you please tell me where we're going?" I asked Colin.

"We're here." Colin panted and wiped his forehead with the sleeve of his T-shirt.

"The old bottling company?" I looked at the building that loomed in front of us. Tilting my head back to get a better view of the towering brick chimneys, I noticed the tops of them were crumpled and uneven. It looked like they could topple over in the lightest breeze. Ivy crawled along the side of the building, weaving its way around windows and gutters.

Colin grinned. "It's more than that now." He chained his bike to a lamppost, and I followed suit. "Come on." He went inside the building, and I followed him.

We stood in the middle of a wide-open room. The ceiling hovered fifty feet above us, a maze of exposed rusted pipes and dark wooden beams. The tile floor beneath our feet no longer displayed a recognizable pattern. Maybe it had been worn down by the heavy steps of hundreds of plant workers. In my mind's eye, I could see the men walking in front of me wearing grimy coveralls and denim train engineer's caps. At least that's what I imagined they might have worn. Our sneakers squeaked on the tile.

"Can I help you?" A deep male voice came out of nowhere, and I jumped.

Colin waved at the voice's owner, a man who looked to be a few years older than my parents. Maybe in his early fifties. He was pencil thin. And even though he sat behind an old wooden desk, I could tell he was tall by the way his too-long legs stuck out from underneath the desk. He had snow-white hair and a black mustache that looked as though he combed it a lot. He wore round glasses, a blue short-sleeve button-down shirt, and a dark green bowtie. On the desk a nameplate sat beside a computer that looked at least fifteen years old. The nameplate read, PATRICK FINNIGAN, CURATOR.

Colin ran over to the man, his sneakers squeaking all the way. Mr. Finnigan grinned as Colin approached. "How's my favorite boy genius this morning?" His voice boomed and echoed through the old factory as though an internal megaphone amplified it.

Boy genius? I glanced at Colin.

"I'm doing okay," Colin said.

"Who's your friend?" Mr. Finnigan asked.

I walked over to the desk, consciously picking up my feet so they wouldn't squeak, and sat down in the other armchair across from the desk.

"This is Andi Boggs, Amelie's niece," Colin said.

"You don't say." Mr. Finnigan held out his hand across the desk, and I shook it. "Amelie told me you and your sister would be living with her. I'm very sorry about your parents."

"Thank you," I murmured. Then I quickly changed the subject. "You know my aunt?"

"You get to know everybody in this town," he said matter-of-factly. "That is, if they stay around long enough. We are really proud of Amelie here—especially now that she's on the faculty at Mike Pike, just like her Grandfather Patterson was. And let me tell you, that's no easy task. But you come from a long line of academics."

"Mike Pike?" I asked, confused. I glanced at Colin for help, but he just grinned back.

Mr. Finnigan smiled. "That's the local-yokel name for Michael Pike University. It's not as stuffy sounding. And I'm sure the university administrators love the nickname."

"My great-grandfather taught there?" I had never heard this bit of info before.

"He most certainly did. Taught there for twenty years in the science department as a biology professor." He stared at me for a moment. I shifted in my seat, wondering what he was thinking. Did he wonder if I possessed any of my great-grandfather's attributes?

Mr. Finnigan blinked. "So enough about that." He clapped his hands together. "What brings you here today? I can't remember the last time you stopped by the museum, Colin."

Colin glanced at me before answering, and I suddenly knew why Colin had brought me to the museum and to Mr. Finnigan. What I didn't know was whether it was a good idea.

Before I could make up my mind, Colin said, "We'd like to find someone."

"Is this person local?"

Colin nodded. "From Killdeer."

Mr. Finnigan pulled a blank piece of paper from his desk drawer and licked the tip of his pen before touching it to the paper. He drew a cluster of squiggles in the corner of the page to get the ink going. When the pen made consistent black doodles, he said, "All right. What do you have for me?"

Colin fidgeted and gave me another fleeting glance. "It's more complicated than that. We're not entirely sure this person exists."

Mr. Finnigan glanced up, his bushy eyebrows making an upside-down V.

"You have to promise not to tell anyone what I'm about to tell you," Colin said in a low voice. I wondered why he felt he had to whisper. Maybe the mice would overhear? I'd bet the old factory was crawling with all types of critters.

I pinched Colin's arm warning him not to say any more. He hadn't mentioned talking about Andora to anyone else. How did we know we could trust Mr. Finnigan? I didn't know him at all.

Colin winced and pulled his arm away from me.

I felt sorry for pinching him, but not sorry enough to want to take it back.

Mr. Finnigan peered at Colin.

Colin rubbed his arm. "We can't tell you unless you promise."

Mr. Finnigan steepled his fingers. "I promise—unless someone is in danger. And then I'll break my promise without thinking twice."

"It's nothing like that," Colin said quickly.

"Okay, I promise I won't tell." Mr. Finnigan picked up his pen again.

"Colin," I hissed.

Colin looked at me while still rubbing the sore spot on his upper arm. "Andi, trust me. Mr. Finnigan knows everything about this town."

"I wouldn't say *everything*," Mr. Finnigan said with false modesty.

"If there is information to be found, he's the one who will find it."

I looked from Colin to Mr. Finnigan and back again. Of course Mr. Finnigan was the man for the job. He was the town curator, for crying out loud. Maybe I hesitated because I was feeling protective of this mysterious Andora that no one knew anything about. Because she shared my name, I felt I had some claim to her ... that I should be the one to look for her. But that was ridiculous. Colin and Mr. Finnigan were only trying to help. "Go ahead."

Colin stopped rubbing his arm, and I noticed a red welt. Maybe I shouldn't have pinched him so hard.

Colin spoke fast, as though I might suddenly change my mind, and told Mr. Finnigan about the trunk in the attic and the story Bergita had told me that morning. As Colin spoke, I watched the older man's face. The curator listened intently, but I couldn't guess what he was thinking. Did he think we were crazy for wanting to find Andora? When Colin finished talking, Mr. Finnigan began jotting cryptic notes on his paper. His handwriting was terrible, but I was used to reading my parents' scientist scrawl and was able to decipher the upside-down script:

A.B. pre-1946?
Probably pre-WW2
Micro news arch

It was gibberish to me.

"What we need to do," he said finally, "is check the news archives from the *Michael Pike Record*, the local paper prior to 1950. That should be easy enough. I would guess from the contents you found in that trunk that we are dealing with a baby or a small child. If a child were born in town back then, the papers would announce it. Newspapers don't have birth announcements anymore—not unless the baby is born to a family that's considered political or important. It's possible your Andora was a wartime baby, which would make her birth very newsworthy indeed. Not too many babies were born in Killdeer during World War Two because all the young men were serving over in Europe or the Pacific."

"Where can we find these archives?" I asked.

"You're in luck." Mr. Finnigan pushed his chair back from his desk. "They're right here in the museum. The newspaper sent them over last year."

Colin gripped the arms of his chair. "Can we see them?"

Mr. Finnigan unfolded himself from under the desk. "Follow me."

As we walked through the building, Mr. Finnigan gave us some background information about the museum.

"This plant represents the largest employer in Carroll County between 1890 and 1932. And it was all thanks to Michael Pike Senior and his famous ginger ale."

"Famous ginger ale?" I paused in front of a life-sized photograph of a plant worker standing by a row of old-fashioned soda bottles making their way down an assembly line. The man wore a gray coverall—just like the ones I'd imagined—and looked bored out of his skull.

Mr. Finnigan stopped mid-stride, and Colin, walking close at his heels, stumbled into him. "Don't tell me you haven't heard of Pike Ginger Ale?" He gestured toward a portrait hanging on the other side of the hallway. The picture showed a dark-haired man with an olive complexion, and the nameplate read, MICHAEL PIKE, SR.

I shrugged.

Mr. Finnigan shook his head sadly.

Colin rubbed his nose where it had rammed into the curator's bony back.

"At one time," Mr. Finnigan said, "Pike Ginger Ale was the most sought-after soda in all of Ohio and parts of West Virginia and Pennsylvania."

"What happened?" I got the feeling Mr. Finnigan liked my interest and, not for the first time, I wondered how many visitors the old bottling plant received. It wasn't exactly Disney World, and Killdeer was at least an hour's drive from the closest interstate. A person would really have to be a fan of Pike Ginger Ale to make the drive.

We moved on to the next two portraits. In the painting on the left, the man's likeness was nearly identical to the man in the first portrait. But the inscription said, MICHAEL PIKE, JR. Next to that was another portrait of, according to the nameplate, Michael Pike, III. The family resemblance was strong between the three men. Dark hair, olive skin, and hooked noses that looked like angry beaks.

"The Crash," Mr. Finnigan began mournfully, "practically cleaned the family out. They held on for a few years, but Pike Ginger Ale never truly recovered. The plant officially closed once Margaret Pike, the fourth generation of Pikes to run the business, finally cut her losses and donated the factory to Killdeer. But the Crash caused the first financial blow to the family business and marked the beginning of the end."

I peeled my eyes away from the portrait of Michael Pike, III. "You mean the Great Depression."

"Of course!" He looked at me suspiciously. "What do they teach kids in schools now-a-days?"

I smiled thinking back to how my fifth grade teacher had spent a whole month talking about the history of rock-and-roll. I guessed Mr. Finnigan would not approve of that teaching unit, even though Cleveland *does* have the Rock and Roll Hall of Fame.

Mr. Finnigan continued, "When the first Michael Pike opened the factory in 1890, it started as a small operation housed in a shed on the back property of his father's home. His father didn't approve and said ginger ale would never take off. He was wrong, of course. Michael began small, selling his drink to local restaurants and families. He soon had a following and enough money to build this factory." He gestured toward the last two portraits. "His son and grandson expanded it after the turn of the century and throughout the Roaring Twenties. You know, your great-grandfather, Patterson Boggs, worked here while putting himself through college."

My eyes widened. "He did?"

Colin didn't seem to have much interest in the old portraits. He stood at the other end of the hallway examining an old piece of machinery. It consisted of three egg-shaped tanks that were as long as I was tall, lying on their sides with copper tubing running from tank to tank. Iron legs held the tanks above the floor.

"What's this?" Colin called out.

"Ahh, I just had that moved here from the factory floor so visitors could have a better look at it. It was a bear to move, and it took four men to do it. It's an old carbonating machine." Mr. Finnigan walked over to Colin. I followed close behind.

"Carbonation is what makes soda pop fizz," I said.

"Exactly," Mr. Finnigan said, pleased. "Seems like you are a chip off of the old scientific block."

I grinned and took a closer look at the machine. Made of heavy copper, it had half a dozen gauges and knobs on it. "This is just one of the many old machines we have here in the building, but this wasn't the big one that the Pikes used when mass-producing ginger ale. It's one of the older ones that Michael Pike Senior used when he was still perfecting his recipe. Do you guys want a tour of the factory?"

"Sure," Colin said. "I haven't seen this place since you moved in."

I shot him an annoyed look. Even though Mr. Finnigan's stories were interesting, my focus was Andora.

"Great, follow me." Mr. Finnigan's black mustache turned up at the corners in a smile.

We backtracked down the hall and returned to the main lobby, where Mr. Finnigan turned in the opposite direction from his desk. "This is the old factory floor." He pointed up toward a rickety set of metal stairs with a DO NOT ENTER sign hanging between the handrails. The last step at the top led into a small room. "That's where the foreman or another boss would sit while the men were working on the floor. That spot allowed one man to supervise the entire floor at one time."

Above where the old foreman used to sit, I spotted a large embossed brass circle with a bird in the middle and PIKE GINGER ALE etched along the sides. The bird stood in stoic profile and reminded me of the seagulls that flew over Lake Erie. "What's that?" I asked.

"That, my dear, is the great seal of Pike Ginger Ale. The bird in the middle is a killdeer, the symbol of Pike Ginger Ale chosen in honor of the town. Killdeers are very special birds."

Colin nodded. "Killdeers live in fields and protect their young at all costs. Their nests are in the high grasses. To keep predators away from their eggs or chicks, they will pretend to have a broken wing to make the predator chase them instead."

I blinked at Colin. He was like a walking Wiki site.

Mr. Finnigan pointed to the assembly line below the killdeer plaque. It was as long as a football field and spread across the factory floor. He explained how the plant workers used to stand in their assigned stations along the line and perform repetitive tasks. Mr. Finnigan walked to each of the workmen's spots and explained their jobs, "The man standing here would measure the ingredients and add them to the vat … this man would monitor the temperature … this man would monitor the bottle washing and remove any bottles that weren't clean enough." Mr. Finnigan walked further down the line. "And finally, this man would put the cap on each bottle, and then the machine would close it with an airtight seal."

I visualized the line of men as if they stood right in front of me, watching the gauges and putting cap after cap on the ginger ale bottles. I wondered which station my great-grandfather had worked. Had he been an ingredients guy, a bottle washer, or a foreman? I made a mental note to ask Amelie if she knew.

I grew anxious to search the archives for any trace of Andora, and I felt sure that if I asked Mr. Finnigan about my great-grandfather, we'd be here all day.

Colin peered inside a box full of old factory tools: screwdrivers, pieces of pipe, and monkey wrenches.

"I'm planning on making a display using those tools. Fascinating, aren't they?" Mr. Finnigan said.

Colin nodded, picking up a hefty-looking monkey wrench.

"You never told us why the company shut down," Colin said. "I mean, if it made it through the Stock Market Crash of 1929, what happened after that?"

To my relief, Mr. Finnigan turned away from the factory floor. "Let's head back to the archives, and I'll tell you on the way." As we made our way, Mr. Finnigan began explaining things to us again.

"The twenties were a time of excess. Michael Pike III enjoyed the profits he received from the family business, which he inherited in full after his father died in '27. But he wanted more. In those days, 'spend now and save later' was the mantra. And Number Three strictly adhered to it."

"Number Three?" I interrupted.

"Michael Pike III. 'Number Three' was a town nickname for him. I'm sure he hated it. He wasn't the kind of man who'd appreciate cutesy names. Anyway, Number Three took out numerous loans to try to expand the business into the root beer and even cola markets, hiring dozens of new employees in a manner of weeks. He threw lavish parties and made dozens of donations to Michael Pike University, which his father started twenty years before in honor of the original Michael Pike. He might have made it, too, but then the Crash happened. Like so many entrepreneurial businessmen, he was too dependent on the soaring price of his stock and the loans from his banks."

Mr. Finnigan shook his head. "They did everything they could think of to save the business. They downsized and produced only ginger ale again, they laid off seventy employees, and they closed the ranks. But the writing remained on the wall. The business probably could have held it together if the public had stayed loyal and continued to drink ginger ale. Unfortunately, people didn't spend money on ginger ale back then because they didn't even have enough money to buy milk for their children. Sometimes they had to send away their children to live with another family or even strangers because they couldn't support them anymore."

"Sounds like you know a lot about this," I said as we re-entered the hallway and walked past the three portraits of the hook-nosed Michael Pikes.

"I grew up in Killdeer, and the bottling company's history is a piece of town lore." He shrugged. "And since we moved the historical society archives in here and opened the museum last year, I've recently completed quite a lot of research on the family. The Pikes were fascinating people."

He stopped in front of another large portrait, this one of a woman in her thirties. "This is Margaret Pike, but everyone called her Peggy. I know her personally. She lives somewhere north of here now, and she's married with kids and grandkids, too."

Colin wandered back to the carbonating machine and started poking at the engine as I stared at the woman's portrait. She had pale skin and red hair that was parted in the middle. Her top matched her cheerful green eyes. As I glanced between her and the three Michael Pikes, I wondered what her mother had looked like.

Colin rejoined us. "So where are those archives?"

We walked down an adjoining hallway lined with checkerboard tiles and dark wood walls. "We put the archives in Number Three's old office. When we started renovating the plant, we found his office to be in remarkable condition. The renovations will continue for quite a while—most of the plant is closed off for the moment, even to me. There are a lot of places that are too dangerous to set foot in." He pulled a key ring from his pocket. The door opened into a room that looked like it once belonged to Number Three's secretary. A photograph of the secretary talking into a black rotary telephone hung on the wall. She wore a crisp suit with a rolled collar and dark movie star lipstick. Her dark hair was arranged in fluffy curls around her small face.

The room was ringed by glass cases filled with artifacts of Killdeer history, from pre-Christopher Columbus arrowheads to Mike Pike T-shirts from the 1990s. I wanted to spend some time mulling over those cases, but the search for Andora came first.

"The newspaper archives are in here," Mr. Finnigan said, as he unlocked a second room that was twice the size of the secretary's office. We entered the room, and Mr. Finnigan flipped the light switch. I gaped.

The archive housed row after row of filing cabinets, which seemed out of place among the faded but still lush Oriental rug and cherry wood paneled walls.

"This is only temporary until we can move the archives into our temperature-controlled room in another part of the factory," Mr. Finnigan explained. "Eventually, we want to restore the office to the way it looked when Number Three ran the plant. The historical society intends to host guided tours of the entire plant after the renovation."

Three alien-looking machines sat in one corner of the room.

"Have you ever used microfilm?" he asked.

Colin and I just stared at him. "Micro *what*?" I asked.

The curator laughed. "Before digital storage, newspapers and other periodicals were copied onto film reels to store and preserve them. You need special machines to read them, and they're called microfilm readers. Those three machines you're staring at are microfilm readers." He sat Colin and me down at two different microfilm readers, and he shuffled over to one of the filing cabinets. "One day we hope to convert the newspapers to computer files. But a huge project like that takes money and a lot more staff than my one-man show."

He opened a long narrow desk drawer, removed four small cardboard boxes, and set them on the table. From the first box, he pulled out a spool of film similar to the kind I'd seen in old movies but much smaller. He held the film carefully and showed us how to wind it through the machine.

"Let's start with 1925 and work our way forward. If you find anything of interest, just hit this button to print it. I wish I could stay and help, but I need to watch the reception desk. Come and find me if you need anything. And I'll come back in a little while to see how you're doing."

More than an hour later, I was still sitting at the microfilm machine, whirling the years back and forth in front my eyes. At first, looking at all of the old newspapers entertained me. I especially liked the ads for Pepsin chewing gum that promised to cure insomnia caused by indigestion. The man in the ad slept soundly under a blanket with an old-fashioned nightcap on his head. No stomachache for him. The Lux laundry soap ad promised to be the perfect soft detergent for washing your most delicate clothing, from sweaters to silk gloves.

After an hour I found my eyes skipping over the advertisements for better dish soap, fresh eggs, and the local grocer's. There was even an ad for Pike Ginger Ale with the proud Killdeer engraved in the middle of the bottle label. It was the same engraving we'd seen on the seal hanging above the factory floor. Every few minutes, Colin called out something about an article he'd found.

Another half hour passed, and Colin was silent. I pivoted in my seat toward him. His eyes were half-closed. "Find anything?" I asked.

He jumped. Then, between yawns, he said, "Not yet."

I glanced at the clock. Eleven thirty. "Let's give it another half hour."

"Sure," he replied, eyelids drooping.

I blinked and leaned closer to the foggy screen, turning the knob to the right to move an advertisement down and out of sight. The Special Reports page drifted into focus. Obituaries, wedding declarations, engagements, and baby announcements covered the page. My tired eyes scanned the words without much thought. Then, something grabbed my attention.

I reread the short article again, moving even closer to the machine so my nose almost touched the screen. My eyes fell on the tiny picture. "Yes!" I hit the Print button.

Colin started at my cry. He had fallen asleep. "What?" His glasses sat crookedly on his nose.

The machine spit out the page on glossy paper. I blew on it, impatient for the ink to dry.

"Listen to this: December 16, 1929. Mr. and Mrs. Patterson Boggs are pleased to announce the birth of a healthy baby girl, Andora Felicity Boggs, early yesterday morning. Andora was born at five a.m. weighing eight pounds, and she was sixteen inches long, possessing all ten fingers and toes. Mother and child now rest comfortably at Carroll Parish Hospital. Andora is the Boggs' first child."

"Wow. She's real." Colin was up out of his seat, reading over my shoulder.

"I know."

"And she's your relative."

"I know."

Colin asked the question that was already plaguing my mind, "What happened to her?"

I squinted at the article, hoping it would reveal Andora's secrets. "I don't know."

We rushed back to the museum entrance to show our find to the curator. I skidded to a stop on the tiles, and Colin ran straight into my back. His poor nose.

Mr. Finnigan wasn't alone. Another man stood over his desk. The second man appeared younger than the curator but older than Amelie by at least a decade. He looked over-tanned and his poofy black hair gave him a couple extra inches of height. I couldn't see the color of his eyes because he wore dark sunglasses even though he was inside.

Mr. Finnigan nodded at the man, agreeing with whatever he'd just said. Then he saw Colin and me approaching. "Did you find something?"

"Yeah," Colin said, waving the paper.

Poofy-Haired Man peered down at us with a slight scowl. He removed his sunglasses, revealing narrowed brown eyes. "Who are you? What are you doing in this place? Why aren't you outside tipping cows, or starting fires, or something equally destructive?" He shuddered.

Was he kidding? I wondered. *No.*

He was a kid hater. Great.

Colin rolled his eyes at me as if to say, *Can you believe this guy?*

I wanted to shoot back, *Who are you? Are you a middle school teacher or something? Shouldn't you go give someone a detention?* But I didn't say anything. I just gave him my best Bethany scowl.

Mr. Finnigan catapulted out of his desk chair and stumbled around the desk. "Dr. Anthony Girard, I'd like you to meet Colin and Andi. They're doing research in the archives." He laughed nervously.

"Really?" Dr. Girard demanded, his tone skeptical.

Mr. Finnigan blundered on as if the speed of his speech would make up for the other man's rudeness. "Dr. Girard is a history professor at Mike Pike. I'm sure he knows your aunt, Andi."

Dr. Girard's voice was sour. "And who might that be?"

"Dr. Amelie Boggs," I answered. I emphasized the "Dr."

"Ah," he said, as if that explained everything. "You're one of the orphans."

Mr. Finnigan shifted uncomfortably. "Dr. Girard, really. I don't … "

Dr. Girard held up a hand, cutting off Mr. Finnigan mid-sentence. "I'm pleased to meet you both." He didn't sound at all pleased. After he straightened, his eyes took on an unpleasant, hard glint. "So what's your wonderful find?"

Like I would tell you now, I thought.

Colin opened his mouth. I elbowed him in the ribs, hard. Too bad I couldn't do the same to Mr. Finnigan.

"They're researching their family histories. Andi discovered that she knows very little about a relative in her genealogy."

Dr. Girard raised an eyebrow. "Really? That's fascinating."

"Dr. Girard has a special interest in local history," Mr. Finnigan explained. "He's written several books on the subject and is one of the best patrons of the archives. The book he's working on right now is about the history of this factory. Maybe he can help you with your own research, Andi."

I squinted at Dr. Girard and said, "No thanks." Then I told Mr. Finnigan that we had to go home.

Colin and I mounted our bikes and pedaled for home. The whole way I thought about Andora and tried to shake off the weird vibe I'd picked up from Dr. Girard.

Andora really existed. I couldn't get that thought out of my mind. But what happened to her? Why doesn't anyone know about her?

When Colin and I arrived back at my house, I told Amelie the good news. Accepting an Oreo she offered me, I asked, "Who is Dr. Girard? Colin and I just met him at the Killdeer Historical Society and Bottling Museum."

She rolled her eyes. "Dr. Girard is one of the most pompous men I've ever met. Unfortunately, the university loves him because he's published several books."

Bethany walked into the living room carrying the box of silk flowers I'd dusted off in the attic.

My mouth fell open. "What are you doing?"

Amelie smiled. "While you and Colin were at the

Bottling Museum, Bethany has been working in the attic."

Bethany flushed. "I'm just moving the stuff that you marked for the sale into the garage."

"I pulled my Jeep out of the garage," Amelie said, "so you kids will have more space for storing the sale items in there. I don't mind leaving it in the driveway until after the garage sale."

"Oh," I said. I couldn't think of anything else to say. I never expected Bethany to help me with this project. "Thank you." I felt Colin watching me.

"Bethany," Amelie said, "why don't you show Andi and Colin what you've been doing while I try to figure out what to make for dinner." She laughed. "I think we're all a little tired of macaroni and cheese from a box."

I followed my sister into the attic. Like she said, Bethany had removed the dozen or so boxes of sale items that we'd stack by the hatch. Even though there was much more to go through and all of the furniture was still there, the attic space already looked larger.

"Right now I'm just stacking the boxes in the garage, but there is plenty of room in there to price stuff and organize it too. I left that blue trunk up here even though I'm assuming you want to sell it."

"I don't," I said quickly. "It belonged to our great aunt. Her name was Andora Felicity Boggs. Colin and I found her birth announcement in the town archives today."

Interest flickered across my sister's face, but when Colin's head popped up through the opening, her interest quickly disappeared.

"Wow!" Colin said in a wheezy breath. "This place is huge! Andi, you're going to have a great room when it's finished."

I had to agree. I slid my eyes to my sister who was now smiling at Colin's praise. "Thanks again for helping."

Her smile disappeared. "Yeah, well, I only did it to get my unlimited texting plan back. And the sooner you move up here, the sooner I get my own room."

I knew that was probably her motivation. But it was a start—a start I was happy to take.

I woke up early again the next morning. All night long, pieces of dreams had disturbed me, leaving a strange prickly feeling—the kind you get when a movie soundtrack turns creepy. I dressed quickly, grabbed a banana and a juice box from the kitchen, and climbed the ladder into the attic. It was six thirty, and Amelie and Bethany wouldn't wake for hours.

The early morning light was fighting its way through the north-facing window. To me, the light of a summer morning always seemed like the best kind of sunray. Its yellow-white glistening nearly blinded me as it lit up the attic. But I liked how friendly and playful that light felt across my arms and face.

Late yesterday afternoon, Colin, Bethany, and I had cleared out the entire northwest corner of the attic— the same corner where I'd uncovered my father's old bed. Mr. Rochester was snoozing on it now. I sat next to him, and the box spring creaked in protest. The cat opened one eye and glared.

Despite the tidy northwest corner and the continuous work of the three of us carrying junk down to the garage, the attic was still a disaster. The worst part was the corner where Colin and I had discovered Andora. Pieces of sailboat wallpaper littered the floor.

I grabbed a garbage bag and began tossing the torn pieces into it. The flutter of paper caught Mr. Rochester's attention, and he jumped off the bed and crouched a foot away from me, concentrating on the colorful pieces with his wide amber eyes and white whiskers. His orange stripes stood upright on his back like soldiers.

The angle of the sunlight allowed me a clear view through the tiny doorway. I squatted in front of it, being careful not to block the light. *Maybe I should clean it out*, I thought. It might make an excellent place to hide things from Bethany. I grabbed the broom that was leaning against a metal rack full of old party dresses, put its business end through the opening, and pulled back hard.

A thick cloud of black dust enveloped Mr. Rochester and me. He yowled before running under the bed. I coughed and stumbled backward, knocking a plastic bin full of wire hangers off an end table. They crashed to the floor.

I froze, waiting for Bethany's outburst from downstairs. When no sound came, I sighed in relief. I knew I didn't want to mess with Bethany before ten in the morning. Not if I valued my life.

One Sunday morning after we'd moved in with the Cragmeyers, I'd made the mistake of waking up Bethany just because I was excited to see my name mentioned in the Akron newspaper.

I'd jumped up and down on her bed. "Bethany, wake up! Look!"

"Leave me alone," she'd growled from underneath her pillow.

It was already after nine, and I'd waited as long as I could to tell her the good news. "Bethany, I won first prize in the Summit County Science Fair! They wrote about it in this morning's paper. My project on photosynthesis beat all the other kids from all the other schools!"

Suddenly Bethany sat straight up in bed, and she would have knocked me in the chin if I hadn't jumped out of the way first. "Andi ... Mom and Dad are dead. So no one *cares* what science experiments you do anymore. They aren't here for you to impress." Then tears appeared in my sister's eyes, and she said, "Now go away."

Clutching my newspaper clipping, I'd silently backed out of her room.

As I recalled that moment, I felt tears threaten at the corners of my eyes. But I shook them away. Andora had to be my top priority now. Not the science fair and certainly not Bethany.

I picked up a flashlight and shone its beam through the small hidden doorway. The ceiling in the crawlspace tapered back into a slant until it finally met the plywood floor. The walls were bare beams without plaster or drywall covering them.

While thinking of all the things I could hide in

that space, I almost didn't see it because it was the same nondescript beige as the plywood it was resting against. I reached into the cubby and pulled out a large manila envelope. Dust balls the size of small kittens flew into the air as I pulled it out of the cubby. And then I sneezed so hard I almost fell over.

I rubbed my eyes and peered at the envelope. It felt dry and brittle like old construction paper. It was blank on the outside, but I could tell something was inside it. It felt heavy in my hand and contained a slight bulge. I slipped my thumbnail under the envelope's sealed flap. The dried glue peeled away easily.

Reaching my hand inside, I pulled out a short stack of old photographs printed on small rectangles of thin cardboard. I counted four in all. The first one depicted a woman whose face reminded me so much of Bethany that I almost dropped it. She stood outside the bottling plant holding a bicycle and smiling cheerfully into the camera. She had Bethany's nose, eyes, and even her chin.

The picture was black and white, so I couldn't make out her hair color. I bet it looked just like Bethany's long blond waves that I envied so much and often prayed would materialize overnight to replace my own pink mop.

I flipped over the photograph; written in precise block letters it read, EMILY, JUNE 1928.

Emily. My great-grandmother.

The next two photographs showed Emily and my Great-Grandfather Patterson standing with that same bicycle in front of the bottling plant. Each photo was taken in June 1928. Patterson, a tall man with laughing eyes and dark hair, had his arm around Emily, and the two smiled at the camera in delight.

The fourth one took my breath away. It was a professional studio photograph of a baby girl in front of a white background. She wore a frilly dress and beamed at the camera with a toothless grin. My eyes darted to Andora's trunk. I'd seen that dress before.

The baby girl looked to be only a few months old, I guessed. Although, I didn't know enough about babies to be sure. Excitedly, I turned over the photograph and read, ANDORA FELICITY, FEBRUARY 1930. My breath caught.

Later that morning, I mulled over Andora's photograph while polishing off the last of my cold strawberry Pop-Tarts. Colin walked into the kitchen with the casebook tucked under his arm. He was wearing the craziest outfit I'd ever seen.

"Ready to get to work?" His voice was muffled.

I took a big gulp of milk. "What are you wearing?"

Colin wore jeans and a striped T-shirt under a hooded sweatshirt, which was all quite normal. But on his head he wore a red bandana underneath a Michael Pike University ball cap. Over his glasses, he wore a pair of chemistry lab goggles. A surgical facemask covered the lower portion of his face, and it was so big that it hid his cheeks, nose, mouth, and chin.

Despite seeing only a small sliver of Colin's face, I

could tell he'd blushed at my comment. Hastily, he removed the mask.

He cleared his throat. "I thought we could work in the attic today."

I blinked. "We will. But what's with the hazmat suit?"

"Bergita wanted me to wear it." He looked down. "I have pretty bad asthma."

"Oh," I said. "But you seemed okay the last couple of days."

He looked up, his eyes chagrin. "Yeah," he agreed, "I was all right at the time. But I had to use my inhaler and drink two gulps of Benadryl after I got home. Bergita found out and had a fit."

"She didn't say anything to me about it."

"Aw, she wouldn't. 'It's my responsibility to take care of myself.'" He repeated the last part as though he'd heard it a hundred times.

I shrugged. "I hope you don't get too hot up there. We'd better find some more fans to use or else you're going to fry." Earlier that morning, the attic had felt stuffy. So I'd changed into a tank top and a pair of shorts. "We can try to pry open the window, too, if we can reach it."

"Thanks," Colin muttered.

Bethany walked into the room wearing boxer shorts and an oversized T-shirt that she uses for pajamas. She jumped when she saw Colin. "Andi! It would be nice if you'd tell me when your boyfriend's coming over." She tossed her glossy blond hair over her shoulder and took a seat beside me, her eyes roving over the break-fast table.

Colin froze, and I glared at my sister.

Bethany rubbed her eyes and noticed Colin's outfit for the first time. "Are you dumpster diving or something?"

Colin shook his head. "I'm working in the attic."

"We could use your help again," I said to Bethany.

She sighed. "We'd better make a bunch of money at the garage sale. I need some kind of reward after being stuck in the attic with the two of you." She grabbed a Pop-Tart and waltzed out of the kitchen.

I'd hoped to find another clue linking Andora to my family. But over the next two days, Colin, Bethany, and I tore apart the attic without uncovering a single trace of her. It appeared that the trunk, the birth announcement, and the lone baby photograph were all that Andora left to this world.

I threw another wire hanger into a box with hundreds of others that would soon go to the garage sale. I had no idea who'd want to buy hundreds of hangers, but Amelie claimed someone would probably buy them. For what? Wire hanger sculptures?

Surrounded by stacks of old flowerpots, Colin sat on the floor beside the hatch and busily sorted piles of papers. I didn't know where Bethany was. She'd said she had "things to do" that day. Whatever that meant.

Colin pushed his goggles higher up on his nose.

"We aren't getting very far with all this." His voice was somewhat muffled by the surgical mask.

"Thanks for reminding me."

"So we have a newspaper announcement about Andora's birth and an old photograph of her, but that's it. Nothing here tells us what happened to her. Searching online has been a waste of time too. So far the only thing we've learned from Googling your name is that there is a town in Italy called Andora; there's nothing about Andora Boggs."

"I know." I tilted one of the five fans that we'd placed throughout the attic so it hit me directly in the face. Outside, it was a beautiful day; it was way too nice to spend all of it inside counting wire hangers.

"We need something more ..." his voice trailed off. Taking his asthma inhaler from his pocket, he took two puffs absent-mindedly.

"What we need to do is get out of here for a while." I thumped him on the back. "You're probably suffering from dust poisoning or something."

Colin looked up at me, his eyes buggy behind those gigantic goggles. "As far as I know, dust can't poison you. It just affects your allergies, which are really just overactive enzymes trying to protect your body ..."

I groaned and helped him stand up. "Let's go."

Downstairs, Colin removed his goggles, surgical mask, and hooded sweatshirt. Now he looked like any other normal kid standing in Amelie's kitchen in jeans and a T-shirt. I laced up my sneakers.

"Where are we going?" Colin asked.

"I want to go back to the museum and talk to Mr. Finnigan. Maybe he can tell us something more."

Outside I rolled my bike out of the garage, which was now packed with furniture and boxes from the attic. How had all of that stuff fit up there? As I stepped out, I heard my sister's voice coming from the front of the house and froze. "I can paint and draw right here. I don't need classes," she said.

The next voice belonged to Bergita. "The classes will help you become a better artist. That's what you want, isn't it?"

"I want to go back home. I miss my life," Bethany said quietly.

"And your parents, I'm sure."

There was silence, and then Bethany said, "I miss them more than Andi does."

My stomach clenched.

"Why do you think that?" Bergita asked.

"Because all she thinks about now is this stupid Andora thing. Who cares about a baby girl who lived a long time ago? I mean, our parents are *dead*." There were tears in her voice. "It's not fair that I miss them more when they obviously loved her more. She was their protégé, the future scientist. All I can do is draw."

"Bethany, everyone grieves differently. When my husband died, I was brokenhearted. But the day after his funeral, I started packing up his clothes so I could donate them to charity. A friend of mine was offended by that. She'd kept her husband's things for years after he died. She thought I was terrible for discarding my husband's stuff so soon. She thought keeping her husband's things proved that she loved her husband more than I loved mine."

I stepped closer to the edge of the garage, but I didn't dare poke my head around the corner.

Bergita continued, "I don't believe your parents loved Andi more. They loved her differently—just like I grieved the loss of my husband differently than my friend did."

Bethany mumbled something I couldn't hear.

Bergita chuckled. "There is a class tomorrow afternoon. Come with me just one time. If you hate it, you never have to go back."

"I guess I have nothing better to do," my sister muttered.

The two of them moved away from the garage, and I ran down the driveway with my bike to meet Colin.

"Where have you been?" he asked.

"In the garage," I said, leaving it at that. "Let's go."

A sign on the bottling company's door said the museum was closed on Saturday afternoons. I parked my bike. "Well, it can't hurt to knock," I said, banging on the door.

Colin and I waited a couple of minutes, and then I knocked again—but a tad softer this time.

"Maybe we should come back Monday," Colin suggested.

Just then, Mr. Finnigan opened the door. His face lit up as he said, "You came back!"

"I know the museum is closed," I said, "but we wondered if we could talk to you about something important."

"Is this about your mysterious Andora?" he asked.

I nodded.

Colin sneezed.

"Then do come in. I've thought a lot about your little mystery over the last few days."

We sat in Number Three's old office munching on Mr. Finnigan's private stash of Double Stuf Oreos. Mr. Finnigan made himself comfortable behind the former ginger ale tycoon's desk, and looked at the photograph of Baby Andora with a magnifying glass.

"This is an original print," he said. "I can tell by the weight of the paper and its general condition."

I dusted Oreo crumbs from my mouth. "We couldn't find any record of her death in the attic or online. And from Bergita's story, it sounds like my family kept her a secret until she vanished. How could a baby just disappear?"

I held back the next question that ran through my head. *How could my family let their baby disappear?*

Mr. Finnigan set the magnifying glass on the mahogany desk. "Times were tough back then. Really tough. But you're right. I don't know how a child, especially one born in such a small community, could simply vanish. I'm sorry. I can't offer any suggestions. This truly is a mystery." Mr. Finnigan thumbed the photograph of Andora. "Do you mind if I hang on to this to help me with the search?"

"Do you think it will help? Can you match it with some pictures in the archives?" Colin asked.

"Maybe," Mr. Finnigan said with a slight catch in his voice.

I looked at the photo in his hand, the only likeness of Andora that I had. "I'd like to keep it with me for now."

Reluctantly, Mr Finnigan handed the photograph back to me. I stowed it between the pages of the casebook inside my mini backpack.

The bike ride home wasn't nearly as enthusiastic as the ride to the museum had been. My legs felt heavy with disappointment, and my eyes passed right over the neighborhood sights. Colin was quiet as we pedaled past Killdeer Middle School, and my mind went back to Andora, the trunk, the elephant block, and her photograph that Mr. Finnigan wanted to keep.

Colin stopped suddenly. I swerved sharply and just missed his back tire.

"Hey!" I said. "What are you doing?"

Colin ignored my protest. "I've got it!"

My heart thumped. "You've got what?"

"I know just what we need. We need someone old—someone who was alive in the 1930s, at the same time as Andora."

"That would be nice, but they'd have to be pretty old now."

"I know just the person." He hopped back onto his bike seat. "Let's go. We need to get home so you can ask Amelie if you can go to church with me tomorrow."

"Ask her what?"

But he was already pedaling away.

Our bike tires spit white gravel into the front lawn. Bergita stood on the Carters' porch with her hands on her hips. "Colin Carter, you get over here right now."

"What did I do?" he asked.

"I told you this morning that your parents would be here for dinner tonight. Now hurry up and get ready."

"I'm sorry, I forgot. Andi and I were—"

"You can tell me what you two were up to later. You know they hate to be kept waiting. They both work third-shift rounds at the hospital tonight."

Colin looked at me. "I gotta go. Can you ask Amelie about church?"

"Why?"

"Colin!" Bergita called.

"I know someone there who might know Andora. Just ask, okay?"

He rolled his bike across the Carters' front lawn.

"I'll ask!" I called after him.

I found Amelie and Bethany in the kitchen. My aunt smiled. "You're just in time for dinner. How does frozen pizza sound?"

"Amelie, you might want to learn how to cook now that you're raising two kids," Bethany said. But there wasn't the typical edge in her voice. In fact, I could be wrong, but I thought my sister might be teasing our aunt.

I plopped down on a stool at the kitchen island. It's where we always ate our meals because Amelie had turned Grandma's dining room into a study.

Amelie must have also noticed Bethany's light teasing tone. Her cheeks twitched as if she were trying to control her smile. Maybe Amelie was afraid that if she looked too happy about her niece's joke, she'd discourage Bethany from trying to be friendlier in the future. "Maybe I should take a cooking class. We could all take one. It would be something fun we could do as a family."

The smile quickly faded from Bethany's face as soon as Amelie said "family." "I don't need to learn how to cook yet."

I swallowed and changed the subject. "Can I go with Colin and Bergita to church tomorrow?"

Amelie dropped her pizza slice onto her plate. "Did you say *church*?"

"Yeah," I said uncomfortably. "He invited me."

"I can't remember the last time I went to church," my aunt said. "Maybe back when you were a baby, Andi."

Bethany eyed me over her pizza. "So you move out to the country and find religion?"

Before our parents died, Bethany and I had regularly attended church back home. I think Bethany used our parents' death as an excuse not to go now. She hadn't been to church in a while. And eventually I'd stopped attending too because everyone treated me like the poor little orphan. Maybe in Killdeer it would be different.

"So what if I have?" I snapped. "Our parents died, and you turned into a brat."

"Andi!" Amelie gasped.

Bethany pushed back from the counter. Her jaw was clenched.

I felt a twist in my gut. *Did I say that because I'm hurt she told Bergita that she misses Mom and Dad more than I do?* I swallowed a lump in my throat. "I'm sorry, I shouldn't have said that."

My sister wouldn't look at me while she put her plate in the dishwasher. My heart sank. I'd just ruined all of the progress we'd made while working in the attic together. She'd never forgive me.

"I'm going to *my* room," Bethany said.

Amelie tapped the counter with her blue fingernails. "Andi, we'll all go to church tomorrow."

"Not me," Bethany said, inching her way out of the kitchen.

Amelie frowned. "Yes, you will—unless you'd rather stay home and mow the lawn?"

Bethany stomped out of the room.

The next morning, Amelie, Bethany, and I piled into the back of Bergita's minivan. Bergita and Colin rode up front. As we headed for the College Church, I thought to myself that a university was a pretty strange place to attend church; but according to Amelie, Michael Pike Senior wanted the chapel built on the campus. And the College Church still held Sunday services even after Michael Pike College had evolved into Michael Pike University.

Bergita smiled in the rearview mirror. "This is the church I attended as a child, Andi. The one where I got in trouble while snatching those cookies."

Separated from the surrounding dorms, classroom buildings, and library by lush green lawns aptly named The Green, the church building was made of gray-purple stone, a unique color I'd seen repeated throughout the campus—even on the newer buildings. I couldn't identify it, so I asked Colin why the stones looked that color.

"It's quartzite," he said. "Quartzite starts out as sandstone, but then it changes due to the heat and extreme pressure caused by the rock's proximity to volcanic belts or earthquake fault lines."

Bethany stared at him. "Do you read the dictionary for fun?"

Colin blushed.

I would have to add geology to my list of sciences to investigate. In the short time that I'd known Colin, I'd learned that he has a wealth of knowledge. He claimed it was from watching *Jeopardy* every night with Bergita, but I wouldn't be surprised if he read a lot of books too.

As we walked from the parking lot to the church, its stone steeple strained toward the heavens, as though trying to reach the highest cirrus clouds above. The dark outline of the heavy iron bell stood out against the late June sky.

Before we entered the church, Amelie pointed at a tiny brick building that looked like a little house behind the church. "You were asking about Great-Grandpa Patterson, Andi?"

I looked in the direction she pointed.

"See that little building over there? It's just an office now, but they used to use it as a guesthouse for special speakers who visited campus. Nowadays the speakers stay in a hotel. But at the time when your great-grandfather taught here, he insisted that guest speakers have a nice place to stay on campus. Since it was his idea, they named the house after him."

We walked over to the building.

"Don't be too long," Bergita called after us. "We're late already."

Mounted on the side of the building, a plaque said, BOGGS GUESTHOUSE, 1950.

"Wow," I said. "It's our name."

Amelie grinned, and even Bethany looked a little impressed.

The inside of the church building didn't appear modern in the least. The odor, a musty mixture of old wood, ancient books, and furniture polish, accosted my nostrils. It smelled like the inside of every historical landmark I'd ever toured during school field trips. From the beamed ceiling to the flagstone entry, everything seemed preserved as though I had stepped back in time. But this would have been much further back than the time of the first Andora—a time of footmen, horse-drawn carriages, and corsets. The thought of corsets made me happy that I didn't live during that era and could wear jeans and a T-shirt to school.

Bergita led us to a pew near the back. The way she chose the seat made me think it was her regular pew. Several people greeted her on the way in. I sat between Colin and Bethany. Bergita and Amelie sat on either end.

Bethany shook her head at me. "You could have dressed up a little for church, Andi."

"I did," I whispered back.

She snorted. My fashionista sister had purposefully chose her outfit this morning—a ruffled skirt and top—while I wore jeans and sneakers. But I'd replaced one of my usual science camp T-shirts with a green button-down shirt.

The pipe organ labored on in the choir loft. Its long heavy tones made me drowsy. My eyes drooped and were half-closed when the call to worship began. The congregation stood and read from the folded bulletins that the ushers had handed to us as we entered the church.

Colin elbowed me in the ribs, and I glared at him, rubbing my side. Colin's elbow was particularly sharp. He ducked his head. "Do you see that lady in the front row?"

"Where?" I stretched my neck, trying to spot the woman in question.

"You'll see her better when we sit down. She's Miss Addy, the person I want you to meet. I bet she's old enough to know something about Andora. Bergita says she's older than dirt."

"I guess that would qualify." I stood on my tippy toes. Half a dozen older adults were standing in the direction that Colin had nodded, but none of them fit his description.

The hymn ended and we sat down. A woman in a canary yellow suit read a passage from the Old Testament.

"First row. Blue hair," Colin hissed.

Miss Addy's shoulders barely cleared the top of the pew. Her hair was gleaming white and styled in an elaborate array of pin curls. Despite my distance from her, I could see her bright pink scalp through the curls.

Bergita poked Colin in the side. "Hush up."

We didn't say anything more after that.

After the service, we filed out with the congregation onto the front lawn. Colin and I hovered by the door waiting for Miss Addy to emerge. Amelie chatted with someone who looked like a professor, and

Bergita gossiped with some friends. Bethany was nowhere in sight.

Miss Addy stepped outside, squinting at the sunshine and supporting herself with a sturdy dark wood cane. She stopped and shook the pastor's hand. The pastor's face opened in a fake smile. Miss Addy punctuated her statements to him with a stomp of her cane. After a few minutes spent critiquing his sermon, she carefully made her way down the stone steps. As soon as she hit the brick walkway, Colin moved in. I followed.

"Good morning, Miss Addy," he said.

She squinted at him. "Colin, the Carter boy," she said to herself. "Where are your parents? I saw Bergita inside but not your mother and father. Don't they have time for Sunday services?"

Colin swallowed. "They had to work at the hospital today."

"On the Sabbath!" she gasped and shook her head. "That's horrible. I'm glad your grandmother has enough to sense to bring you in spite of your parents. Children should grow up in church. There's no other acceptable way." She spotted me hovering behind Colin. "And who is this?"

Colin stepped out of the way, and I grimaced. There went my human shield.

"This is Andi Boggs, Amelie's niece."

"You're the child who lost her parents in that plane crash down in the tropics, aren't you? I thought there were two of you."

"I have an older sister named Bethany. She's here too," I said.

"That's good. We don't see much of your aunt." Her small, dark eyes bore into me. "What is your name again?"

"Andi."

She shook her head. "Andi's not a fit name for a girl. Parents today think they have the license to name their children whatever they wish. Ridiculous. You hardly hear any good solid names anymore. I miss names like Ruth or Mary or Rebecca. It's all Apple, Mango, and Pear these days. What, do people think they are making a fruit salad instead of naming a child? My land, everyone has a strange, off-putting name. It's shameful."

"*Andi* is short for *Andora*."

Miss Addy let out a puff of air. "What did you say?"

"My full name is Andora Boggs."

"Oh, well, that's … better." Her hand fluttered to the floral scarf around her neck. "Well, I must find Mrs. Chesterton. She promised to take me home. They won't let me drive anymore, you see." She lost her grip on her cane, and it fell to the ground.

I bent to pick up the cane and handed it to her. "Does that name mean something to you? Is there something you can tell us about the Andora Boggs who was born in December 1929?"

Miss Addy's eyes widened. "Andora? No, I … sorry, I really must go now. I hope to see you and your aunt here at church more often. Good day." She whirled around without another word and scurried away faster than I would have thought possible, holding her cane just above the ground. She never looked back.

I glanced at Colin. "Well, we know one thing for sure."

Colin frowned. "What's that? She didn't tell us anything."

"You're wrong. Her reaction told us a lot. I'm willing to bet Miss Addy knows exactly who Andora was. But for some reason she doesn't want to talk about it."

After church, we ate lunch in the university's cafeteria. In the large dining hall, summer students shouted to each other across the room. We sat at a long table beside a huge window. On either side of our table, students ate, studied, and laughed at equally long tables. The window gave a clear view of the campus grounds and the church. The pastor stood on the front steps of the church, locking the doors.

I took a big bite of my pizza.

"Colin just told me about your run-in with Miss Addy," Bergita said.

A piece of cheese lodged in my throat, and I gulped down half of my Coke.

"I hope that's okay," Colin said quickly. "Bergita knows Miss Addy better than we do, and she might know why Miss Addy reacted that way."

I swallowed and gave Colin a pointed look. "What do you think about it, Bergita?"

"Don't know. But it makes me think you've stumbled onto something. Miss Addy is a straightforward kind of lady. She says what she thinks and doesn't care who hears her. I bet she knows all about your Andora."

The screech of a chair scratching across the linoleum floor caught my attention. I looked behind me and saw Dr. Girard leaving a table packed with students.

I glanced at Colin, but he was digging into his cheeseburger and hadn't noticed.

Bergita started telling us a story about the time when my dad was fourteen and fell off the roof of our house. "He was always getting into or climbing onto something—"

My eyes followed Dr. Girard as he threw away his trash and dropped off his tray on his way out of the dining hall.

"I have to use the bathroom," I interrupted.

Bergita blinked. "Sure thing, honey. You go right ahead."

Bethany, who was bent over her sketchbook, sighed. "Andi, you're not in preschool. You don't have to make a public service announcement when you have to use the potty."

I jumped up from my seat and followed Dr. Girard. Outside the cafeteria, I spotted him walking toward the church. If I followed him, I'd need to cross directly in front of the big window where my family and the Carters were eating lunch. Dr. Girard had almost reached the steps of the church. I hoped Bergita kept the group occupied with more of her stories.

I tailed him, not sparing even one glance behind me. What was Dr. Girard up to, and why had he left so quickly when Bergita said Andora's name? Was it a coincidence? Something told me it wasn't. He'd reacted to her name. I knew it.

Instead of going up the church steps, Dr. Girard followed the brick sidewalk on the left side of the building. He walked with long, confident strides and breezed right past the church and headed toward more academic-looking buildings. Passing students greeted him along the way; whenever he stopped to talk to them, I ducked behind a nearby bush or trash can.

At last, he arrived at a stone building with the name WHIT HALL carved in stone above the door. I hid around the corner of the building, with one eye peeking out and watching his every move. Dr. Girard used a key card to enter the hall. He threw the door open with a flourish and waltzed inside. I sprinted for the door and caught it just as it was about to close.

Whit Hall's main entryway had a vaulted glass dome for a ceiling and polished marble floors. I shivered. The thick stone walls and marble floors kept the building a chilly temperature.

Dr. Girard was long gone. I stumbled forward, unsure of which way I should turn. Then I saw the building directory bolted to the wall. Under HISTORY DEPARTMENT it read, DR. ANTHONY GIRARD, DEPARTMENT CHAIR, ROOM 102B. A friendly arrow pointed me in the right direction. How convenient.

The rubber soles of my sneakers squeaked on the glossy marble floor. So I took them off and carried them in my hand. Walking on the cold marble barefoot felt like tip-toeing on ice. I moved stealthily down the hallway.

When I reached the history department suite, the

outer door was standing ajar and the lights were on inside. I slipped inside. A generic-looking reception area with two large connected desks dominated the front of the suite. On both desks sat computers and stacks of files. A hunter green sofa with two matching armchairs sat in one corner. A fake dusty palmetto plant sat between the chairs. The room possessed about as much appeal as a dentist's waiting room.

Dr. Girard's voice floated down the hall that led deeper into the department. I couldn't make out any of his words. So I moved around the reception desk and peeked down the hallway. Counting four or so doors down the darkened hallway, my eyes settled on the only one with light streaming under it.

I inched along the wall, hopping from doorframe to doorframe and working my way toward the lit office. The door stood open just a crack. When I was two doors away from my target, I could hear Dr. Girard clearly.

"I'm telling you, Miranda, this has all the makings of a small-town exposé." He paused. "I know I need more proof. But I'm on it. We could turn this into a series on children from the Great Depression. Tom Brokaw made a mint off of *The Greatest Generation*, so why can't I?" Another pause. "Yes, yes, you're right. I won't get carried away. Have you heard any word?" Pause.

Dr. Girard had to be talking on the telephone.

"Excellent, excellent. So they're interested." Pause. "I can have the full proposal to you by the end of the month." His voice sounded angry. "Well, you want me to check out the facts, don't you? That will take time.

All I have are rumors and old newspaper clippings." He sighed. "I don't want to approach the family just yet. But I will in good time. All right. I'll be in touch." I heard a soft click as though he'd just replaced the handset. Then I heard the soft squeak of body weight shifting in a chair. My heart leapt into my throat.

Dr. Girard began whistling an unrecognizable tune, and suddenly the light went out in his office. I looked up and down the hallway for somewhere to hide. Nothing. I quietly ran back to the reception area clutching my sneakers to my chest. Scooting under one of the massive reception desks, I tucked the rolling desk chair in after me just as Dr. Girard's whistles filled the hallway. His melody passed overhead, the whole room darkened as he flipped off the light switch, and I heard the soft click of the suite door as it closed.

I relaxed as I peek out from under the desk. I would wait a few minutes just to make sure Dr. Girard was really gone before I left.

Then, to my horror, the door handle moved and the door cracked open again.

"Good morning, Joan. What are you doing here on a Sunday afternoon?" Dr. Girard asked.

"You know a secretary's work is never done. I thought I'd just finish up some projects while the office is quiet. I leave for Hawaii on Friday."

"I hope my book proposal is one of those projects," said Dr. Girard.

"It is," she said.

The secretary? That meant I was probably hiding under Joan's desk. I had to move. The doors lining the hallway were all closed. I prayed one of them was also unlocked.

The door to the suite opened a little wider, and I could see Dr. Girard through the crack. I had to move now. I ran to the first door at a low crouch and tried the handle. I was in luck, the door was unlocked. I slipped inside the room just as Joan turned on the lights in the reception area.

I leaned against the closed door and listened to the muffled sounds of Joan moving around the main office. I had to get out of here. Who knew how long she planned to stay? I looked around and found I wasn't hiding in a professor's office but a workroom. An enormous copier stood on one side of the room, and the other side was filled with floor-to-ceiling shelves holding reams of paper in every color I could imagine.

Outside the workroom, rock music started playing. That was good because it would be harder for the secretary to hear me, but it was also bad because I might not hear her if she decided to make copies.

My eyes fell on a window.

Duh! A window.

It was conveniently located for pesky kids and cat burglars alike. A long table covered with office supplies like tape dispensers, staplers, and stacks of legal pads sat underneath it. I climbed onto the table, taking care to be as quiet as possible. I placed my sneakers beside me on the tabletop and unlocked the window. It opened easily. With care, I popped out the screen and stuck my head through the opening. Luckily, the history department was located on the first floor of the building. Below me, I spotted a bed of flowers, but I didn't see anyone around. The secretary must have opened her window too because the rock music seemed to be even louder outside. I wouldn't have to worry too much about being quiet. Which was good.

I threw my sneakers onto the lawn and shimmied leg-first out the open window, taking care to grab the screen as I fell. I landed on my rear in a patch of pink sweet alyssum. Jumping up and off the flowers, I grimaced when I realized that I'd accidentally ground many of them into the red mulch. I wiped the mulch and dirt off my backside, closed the window, and replaced the screen. That would have to do.

I sidestepped around the building and away from the secretary's open window. When I was several yards from Whit Hall, I broke into a run back to the cafeteria. Inside the dining hall, I stopped to catch my breath. After calming myself down with several big gulps of air, I walked up to our table where Amelie waited alone.

"What took you so long?" she asked. "Are you feeling okay? I sent Bethany to look for you, but she said you weren't in the bathroom."

"I ..." I bit my lip. I didn't want to lie to my aunt, but I didn't want to tell her about chasing Dr. Girard across campus and being trapped in the History Department either. "I went to a different bathroom," I said.

Amelie looked relieved. "As long as you're okay."

"I'm sorry for holding everyone up."

She smiled. "It's all right. But I hope you didn't want dessert because everyone else is waiting out by the van."

I didn't tell Amelie that I wanted to go to the bathroom first because now I really did need to use it.

When we got home, Bethany went straight to our room and packed up her paints, charcoals, and brushes for the weekend art class she promised to take with Bergita.

I sat on the edge of my bed and watched her.

"I don't need an audience," she muttered.

I opened my mouth to tell her I wasn't Mom and Dad's favorite, but I closed it again. How could I tell her that without revealing that I'd overheard her and Bergita talking yesterday?

Amelie poked her head in the room. "I'm so happy you're taking this class, Bethany."

"It's just one class. If I don't like it, I'm not going back."

"Fair enough," my aunt said.

Bethany and I both stared at her in surprise. We were used to being told that we had to participate in things and see them through to the end. We weren't allowed to quit if we didn't like something. Our parents had never given us a choice.

"So what are you up to this afternoon, Andi?" Amelie asked.

I shrugged. My thoughts were still jumbled from my near-escape from the History Department.

She smiled. "That's okay. You don't have to be up to anything. Sundays were made for being lazy."

After Bethany left for her class, I wandered around

the house until I ended up in my aunt's study—the one that had once been a dining room. She'd lined the walls with floor-to-ceiling bookcases. Bookshelves were even installed above the two large picture windows.

In the middle of the room stood a huge dark wood desk and an old-fashioned wooden desk chair. Amelie's laptop hummed in the middle of the desk. In the far corner, next to one of the windows, she'd placed a purple armchair and matching ottoman. A floor lamp with a black-fringed shade hovered over the back of the chair. Throughout the cozy room, I spotted little knick-knacks and trinkets from my aunt's travels and adventures.

I curled up in the purple chair feeling an odd mix of guilt and apprehension. I knew I felt guilty because I hadn't been completely honest with my aunt, and I was apprehensive about Dr. Girard's phone conversation. What did it mean? Did he want to include Andora in his book? Who had he been talking to?

I left the study and found Amelie in the middle of the living room. Wearing a tank top and cotton yoga pants, she was twisted into a small ball. Her hands, pressed flat on her yoga mat, held her body in the air. Her glasses slid down to the tip of her nose. She opened one eye and spotted me watching her.

Slowly she lowered herself to the floor. "Do you want to try?"

I sat on the green plaid couch. "I could never do that."

Amelie bent her body in half and held on to her feet. "Sure you could. It just takes practice." She straightened.

"Do you know a person named Miranda?"

Amelie raised an eyebrow. "Miranda? No, I don't think so. This isn't another unknown relative, is it? Because one is plenty."

"No, I just heard her name mentioned and wondered who she was."

Amelie lifted her right leg behind her head. "Who'd you hear it from?"

"Dr. Girard."

Her eyebrows shot up. "When was that?"

I played with the hem of my T-shirt. "After church when I said I was going to the bathroom, I didn't really go. I followed Dr. Girard."

Amelie dropped her body to the floor and sat up on her knees. "Spill it."

When I looked at Amelie's face, I knew this moment was important. I hesitated, torn between lying and coming clean. I opted for the truth.

Amelie went very still. "I know you're a curious kid, but ..."

"I know. I'm sorry." I smoothed my T-shirt's invisible creases.

"Why'd you follow him?"

"I don't know exactly. He ran out of the cafeteria so quickly, I thought maybe he'd overheard Bergita talking about Andora and that's what made him leave."

Amelie's eyebrows shot up again, and her brow wrinkled as if she were trying to come to some type of decision, like how many weeks she should ground me for lying. "Why would Dr. Girard care about Andora?"

I shrugged. It was the same question I'd asked myself

a dozen times while sitting in my aunt's office. I didn't know why; but at the same time, I knew I was right.

Amelie's freckled brow smoothed. "Thank you for telling me the truth, but consider this a warning: I will not accept lying from either of you girls. And please, don't go running after strange men you don't know. Do you know how dangerous and stupid that is?"

I nodded solemnly.

She returned to her stretches. "What was the name of that woman Dr. Girard mentioned?"

"Miranda," I said, feeling relieved that she wasn't angry with me.

Amelie lowered her leg and rolled her eyes. "I know who Miranda is now."

"You do?"

"Well, that's not entirely true. I've never met the woman." She put her left leg behind her head.

"Who is she?"

"She's Dr. Girard's literary agent. He's written a couple of books about Ohio history, and she helped him get them published. I have both of them in my study." She flipped onto her stomach. "You can look at them, if you want. Actually, both of Dr. Girard's books are well written, and he has some interesting theories on local history." She rested her elbows on the floor.

I returned to the study and walked along the bookcases, tapping my fingers against the dusty spines. As far as I could tell, there wasn't much organization to the bookshelves. Russian authors rested next to Brazilian ones. Mathematicians stood close to philosophers. In my parents' home office, each book subject was divided and alphabetized within an inch of its life. Any time I'd taken a book from my parents' collection up to my room, they'd known about it. I bet Amelie wouldn't notice if I took a whole shelf of books from her library.

However, Amelie knew exactly where she'd left Dr. Girard's books. They were on the bottom shelf of the third bookcase to the right of the door—right where she'd said they'd be.

I knelt in front of the shelf and plucked out the books to get a better look at their covers. The first book had a photograph of a brick farmhouse on it, and the title read, THE MIDDLE CLASS PIONEER OF 1800. Dr. Girard's name was printed in big white letters at the bottom of the cover.

On the second cover, Dr. Girard's name appeared in even bigger red letters above a picture of a woman wearing a red bandana on her head and leaning against a pile of black rubber tires. The book was called *Women in the Rubber Plants*. I read the dust jacket, which explained that it was a book about women working in the tire factories in Akron while the men fought during World War Two.

I was disappointed. I'd hoped to find a book like *Lost Children of Ohio* or *Family Scandals of the Great Depression*. Something that would tie Dr. Girard to my search for Andora. As much as I wanted Dr. Girard to have something to do with the Andora mystery, maybe I'd misjudged him. He could have been talking to Miranda about any local family. It didn't have to be mine.

The doorbell rang.

"Andi, can you answer that?" Amelie called out.

I sighed and stood up, putting Dr. Girard's books back on the shelf where I'd found them. Amelie couldn't answer the door because she'd wrapped herself into a pretzel and would snap off a toe if she tried. And she tells me yoga is relaxing.

I opened the front door and gaped.

"Just the person I want to see," Dr. Girard said in a fake-friendly voice.

"Andi, who is it?" Amelie called. I heard a thump from the living room, and a few seconds later, Amelie stood beside me. "Anthony? What are you doing here?" She looked from Dr. Girard to me.

"And hello to you too, Amelie." He eyed her outfit. "I see you're making the most of your summer break."

"I'm trying to. Can I help you with something?"

Dr. Girard smiled without showing any teeth. "In truth, I'm not here to talk with you." Dr. Girard adjusted the collar of his polo shirt. "I'd like to speak with your niece, Andi."

Amelie blinked. "Andi? Why?" Her brow wrinkled. "It's not because—"

"I met Dr. Girard at the Bottling Museum last week. Remember? I know I told you that, Aunt Amelie," I said in a rush because I knew she was about to ask Dr.

Girard if he knew I'd followed him into his office during lunch.

"That's right," Dr. Girard said. "And I was impressed by her keen interest in local history." He smiled at me. "I thought she might be able to help me with my latest book project."

"Which is?" Amelie asked.

"A book on children of the Great Depression."

I had been right. Dr. Girard had to be here because of Andora. But how did he know that Andora lived during the Great Depression? Mr. Finnigan. He must have told Dr. Girard about Andora.

"Can I come inside to discuss this matter further?"

Amelie winced. "Why don't you two talk outside on the front porch?" She gave Dr. Girard a small smile. "Andi and her sister are cleaning out the attic, so the house is a mess right now."

Dr. Girard pulled at his collar, his hair was starting to curl up from the humidity. "Very well."

"Go ahead and take a seat, Anthony. I'll get you two some iced tea," Amelie said.

I stepped onto the front porch, and Dr. Girard sat down in the rocking chair at the end of the porch. I perched on the porch swing, kicked off the porch floorboards hard, and the swing flew back with a protesting creak. I swung my legs up on the bench and let it rock me back and forth like the waves that carried the red and blue sailboats along my father's wallpaper.

Dr. Girard cleared his throat. He pulled a tiny memo pad out of his jacket pocket. I wrinkled my nose when I noticed he was wearing black socks and sandals.

"So, Andi, this should be quick. I have just a few questions for you to answer. I don't want to take up too much of your time."

Sure you don't, I thought unkindly. I tried to squelch the irritable thoughts. My mother would have said that I make too many snap judgments and I should give Dr. Girard the benefit of the doubt, whatever that meant. He already had my doubt.

"I must admit that I was surprised to see you and your friend Kevin in the museum on such a beautiful summer day. I imagine most of your peers were out swimming or playing baseball."

"Colin," I corrected.

"Of course. Colin. I apologize," he said smoothly. He pulled a pen from his shirt pocket. "What brought you to the Killdeer Historical Society?"

"Colin wanted me to see it." If we were going to talk about Andora, Dr. Girard would have to mention her first.

"Ah! Should I be talking to Colin, then?"

I shrugged. "If you want to. He lives right next door." I pointed toward the Carters' house.

He tapped his chin with a forefinger. "I remember Mr. Finnigan mentioned that you children wanted to search for a relative in the historical society archives. Is that right?"

The hair on my arms stood up on end. My porch swing lost its momentum and slowed to a gentle sway. I let a leg fall over the side and gave the floorboards another push with my toes.

"Can you tell me about this relative?"

"I don't really know anything about her."

My mind was screaming, *I was right! He is interested in Andora!* But I did my best to keep a calm expression on my face.

Dr. Girard clicked his pen. "Wasn't she the real reason Colin took you to the museum?"

"How would you know that?"

He smiled coolly. "Mr. Finnigan is a good friend of mine."

I looked at my leg dangling from the swing.

Dr. Girard wrote something in his tiny memo pad again. "You know, Andi, I could really use your help."

"You could?" I asked.

"I don't know how much your aunt has told you about me ... "

"Just that you're a history professor at Mike Pike."

He winced. "I see you've learned the local nickname for the university. Anyway, for you to have an appreciation for research at such a young age, you must be a perceptive, intelligent girl. Your aunt may not have told you, but I'm a bit of an expert in Ohio history, and I've written books on the topic."

"She did." I didn't add that I'd been leafing through those very books the moment he rang our doorbell.

"Excellent. I'd like to tell you about my project on Depression-era children, and then you can tell me yours."

I sat up straighter in my seat. My feet hit the wooden boards of the porch with a thud. I swallowed hard. I didn't tell him that I already knew he was writing a book about children from the Great Depression because I'd overheard him talking to his agent about it. "Why do you think I'd know anything about that?"

"Mr. Finnigan has assisted me in my research for years. He mentioned that you visited the museum to search the archives for a lost relative born in 1929, and the relative's name was Andora."

My heart raced. What could he tell me about Andora? Did he know what happened to her? I had to know. "What do you know about Andora?"

He gave me a wry smile. "Why don't you tell me how you learned about her first?"

I wondered if I should tell him what I knew. If I didn't, there was no chance he'd tell me what he knew about Andora. I was pretty sure Dr. Girard wouldn't offer information without getting something in return. I tried to look him in the eye, but he was wearing his dark sunglasses again.

And then I made my decision. It was the only option I had if I wanted to learn more.

It took only a few minutes for me to tell Dr. Girard what little information I was willing to share. I told him about the trunk, the baby clothes, the wooden blocks, and the birth announcement. I said nothing about the photograph of Andora or the encounter with Miss Addy.

Amelie appeared on the front porch with a tray of iced tea and Girl Scout Cookies. She simply raised her eyebrows when she heard me talking to Dr. Girard about Andora.

The history professor accepted a perspiring glass of iced tea from my aunt and removed his sunglasses. He took a gulp from his drink and said, "I'd like to see the items in the trunk and the cubby where you found the trunk."

"Umm ..." I stalled and chewed the inside of my

cheek. "The attic is a mess right now. I mean, it's worse than downstairs. It'll take me some time to move stuff around so you can reach the cubby."

"I don't mind a mess." He glanced down at his small memo pad and flipped through the pages. He'd taken notes so detailed that it seemed he'd written every word I'd said.

Part of me wanted to keep Andora to myself. I found her first. I shared her name. And what had Dr. Girard given me in return? "So what do *you* know about Andora?" I asked.

Dr. Girard waved his hand. "Not much. That's why I'm here. Patrick Finnigan told me about her because he knew I was working on this piece about children during the Great Depression, and he thought she'd be an interesting addition to my book."

I felt myself deflate. "But you said you do know something about her."

He nodded and smirked. "And I will tell you what little I know just as soon as I have a look at that trunk."

I gritted my teeth.

"I'll stop by tomorrow afternoon. That should give you plenty of time to tidy up the attic." He rose to his feet and brushed imaginary crumbs off his pants.

With my foot, I pushed off the porch floorboards hard, sending the old swing careening backward.

Amelie stood. "Andi didn't agree to show you the attic yet, Anthony."

I still wanted to know what Dr. Girard knew about Andora, and showing him the attic might be my only means of getting that information. "It's all right, Amelie," I said, bringing the swing to a halt with my foot. I stood and said, "Two o'clock tomorrow should be fine, Dr. Girard."

Amelie turned to me. "Are you sure?"

"Yes," I said with more conviction than I felt.

Amelie nodded and turned back to Dr. Girard. "What exactly do you plan to do with the information Andi has shared with you, Anthony?"

Dr. Girard's thick brows waggled above his dark sunglasses. "Like I told your niece when I arrived, I am currently working on a new project about children during the Great Depression. It will include letters and short biographies of children from all over the state of Ohio. If we can find enough information about Andora to include her, she would be one of two dozen children mentioned in the book. I've wanted to write this book for a long time. If I wait too much longer, many of the elderly adults who were children in the 1930s will be gone. I'll return tomorrow afternoon, Andi." He stood and grabbed a cookie from the tray before he left.

Colin froze where he stood in our yard as Dr. Girard headed in the opposite direction and down the sidewalk toward his car. As Dr. Girard drove away, Colin ran up the porch steps.

"I hope you won't be disappointed by what you learn from Dr. Girard, Andi," Amelie said before she went back inside.

"Is that who I think it was?" Colin removed his glasses and wiped them on his T-shirt.

"Yep," I said. "And he'll be back tomorrow afternoon."

Colin grabbed a handful of Girl Scout Cookies from the tray. "Tell me everything." He pulled the casebook from his backpack.

I told Colin about my encounter with Dr.Girard. And after a moment's hesitation, I told him about following Dr. Girard into his office earlier that day. Colin wrote down every word.

During my story Colin had interrupted me every few seconds with questions, but suddenly he got quiet.

"What is it?" I asked.

"Why didn't you tell me you followed Dr. Girard?"

"I don't know. I planned to tell you. I wanted to think it through first."

"We could have thought it through together. I thought we were a team." He frowned.

"It's no big deal." I said.

"It is a big deal," he insisted. "It makes me think you don't trust me. And I could have helped you follow Dr. Girard, too."

"It's not like we both could have gotten up and said we were going to the bathroom without it looking like something was up."

Colin snapped the casebook closed. "I was the one who took you to the museum in the first place. If it hadn't been for me, you wouldn't even know Dr. Girard."

"You can't take credit for that. We met him there by accident."

Colin folded his arms.

Bergita's van turned into the Carters' driveway, and Bethany jumped out of the van. She was smiling as she ran across the lawn, gripping her art case. She pulled up short when she saw Colin and me frowning at each other. "What happened? Did you find out Andora was sold to the circus?"

Colin ran down the steps and back to his own house. Bethany watched Colin go. "I guess I'm not the only one who gets tired of you."

Before I could respond, she slipped into the house.

That night, I sat in the kitchen long after I should have gone to bed, waiting for Bethany to fall asleep. I didn't want to talk to her about Colin, or Andora, or most of all about our parents.

I wiped a damp rag over a silver picture frame that I'd found under the bed in the attic. Carefully, I removed the photograph of Andora from the safety of the casebook and placed it in the frame. I set the framed picture on the kitchen counter.

"Who are you? What happened to you? Where are you?" I asked.

Andora stared back at me but said nothing. I hadn't expected an answer, but I wouldn't have turned one down either.

Mr. Rochester jumped on the counter and nosed the frame.

"Mr. Rochester, you're not supposed to be up here."

"Meow!"

I petted his back. "I promise I won't tell as long as you won't tell Amelie how late I stayed up."

The cat nudged my hand with his head, and I took that as him saying we had a deal.

I picked up the frame and turned off the kitchen

light. With the lights off in my own house, I could see into Colin's house next door. I tip-toed to the window, clutching the picture to my chest. Through the window, I saw the Carter family's den. Colin's parents were home. The slim, blond couple sat side by side on the couch reading the newspaper. Colin stepped into the room and asked them something. Colin's father shook his head. Colin's face fell. He turned and left the room. His mother never looked up from the paper.

I swallowed as I remembered the last time I'd burst into my parents' study on the night before they left for their last trip to Central America.

"Mom and Dad! I got an A+ on my science test! Mr. Pearce said it was the best score in the class!" I held the test out in front of me for them to see.

"That's nice, honey," my mother said. Then she'd turned and asked my father, "Art, have you seen my field guide to succulents?"

He was bent over his microscope. "I hope you didn't leave it at the office. We don't have time to swing by campus on the way to the airport."

"Do you want to see my test?" I asked.

"Later, Andi," Mom said.

My arms fell to my side as I listlessly held the test in my left hand.

Dad didn't look up from his microscope. "We can see it before we leave. Your mother and I are taking the red-eye tonight."

I crumpled the edge of my test in my hand.

One of Bethany's paintings hung on the wall behind

Mom's desk. Bethany didn't understand. I wasn't the favorite child at all, not even close.

I'd woken up the next day with the test under my pillow. They never did see it.

I went to bed then feeling sorry for Colin, and feeling angry at and sorry for myself.

There was a knock on the front door a little after eight the next morning. Colin stood on the other side of the door wearing his hazmat suit.

"Hi. I'm surprised you're here," I said.

"I'm here to help with the attic. I said I would help." He acted sheepish.

I folded my arms. "If you don't want to, it's okay. It's close to being done now. I can do the rest by myself."

"Listen, Andi," Colin said. "I'm sorry about how I acted yesterday. I know what Bergita would have thought if she'd seen it."

"I have a few guesses, too." I dropped my arms to my sides.

He swallowed. "I'm not included in a lot of stuff. You know, at school. The kids just think I'm some weird nerd who hangs out with his grandmother and her friends." He reddened. "So when you didn't ask me to follow Dr. Girard, I thought that maybe you ... had come to the same conclusion."

I thought about what it must be like to be an only child whose parents are gone all the time. Even when they were still alive, my parents weren't around that often. But at least I'd had Bethany. She wasn't much of a companion to me now, but we'd been closer when we were younger. And even now, she was at least someone close to my age.

I grinned at Colin and hoped the grin was enough to let him know that I'd forgiven him. I spun around, leaving the door opened behind me. "You coming or what? The attic won't clean itself."

At precisely two o'clock, the doorbell rang. This time I peered through the peephole first and saw Dr. Girard standing on the other side of the door, holding a brown leather briefcase in his hand. "It's him," I told Amelie and Colin.

I opened the door.

"Andi," he greeted me. "It's so good to see you again. Let's go straight to the attic, shall we?"

Amelie looked like she was about to say something, so I jumped in, "Okay." The sooner I showed Dr. Girard the trunk and its contents, the sooner he would tell me what he knew about Andora. At least I hoped he would.

Since space in the attic was tight for more than three people, Amelie volunteered to stay behind. The rest of us trooped upstairs. I climbed up the attic ladder first, followed by Dr. Girard and then Colin. The older man knocked his head on the side of the hatch and swore under his breath. I covered my mouth to keep from laughing, but Colin laughed from below.

Once upright, Dr. Girard ducked to avoid the low spots in the ceiling.

Bright sunlight poured into the attic through the open and recently washed window. I grimaced as I remembered how it took us ten attempts with glass cleaner and about forty paper towels to remove the grime off the glass. A light breeze floated in through the window, but the attic still felt stuffy. I switched the knobs on the fans to maximum power. Dr. Girard tugged at his button-down collar.

"Here's what we found," I said.

I showed Dr. Girard the little blue trunk, which I'd placed on a small end table. He pulled a pair of reading glasses out of his shirt pocket and slid them onto the bridge of his nose. Gently, he lifted out the china doll and placed her on the table beside the trunk. Then he examined the clothes and the wooden blocks.

"Where'd you find it?"

Colin pointed to the cubby door and then opened it by tugging on the string we'd looped through the space where a doorknob had once been. Dr. Girard squatted in front of the cubby, and Colin handed him a flashlight. I sat on top of a nearby dresser and waited.

"So, someone hid the trunk," Dr. Girard murmured with a small smile. After a few minutes, during which he knocked on all of the walls inside the cubby and felt around the dusty floor, he leaned back on his heels. Then Dr. Girard stood and wiped his hands on the clean rag that Colin offered to him. His mouth was turned down. "You didn't find anything else in there?" he asked, swiping a dust bunny off his knee.

I thought about the framed photograph of Andora sitting on my nightstand downstairs.

"This is all *we* found," Colin said.

I smiled at him gratefully. I had been alone when I found the photograph of Andora, and so what Colin said was technically the truth.

Dr. Girard walked back to the end table. "These items are certainly consistent with the time period." The professor hunched over the small trunk like a vulture. Then he straightened as a peculiar look crossed his face.

The look passed quickly, and I wondered if I'd just imagined it.

"Are you sure you don't have *anything else* to show me?" He turned from me to Colin and back again.

"We're sure." I would make a decision about showing him the photograph and telling him about Miss Addy after he told me what he knew, not before. It was Dr. Girard's turn to share some information with Colin and me.

Dr. Girard picked up the china doll, turned her over, and looked under her dress as if instead of doll-sized pantaloons, the skirt might be hiding some great secret to Andora's identity. He placed the doll back inside the trunk on top of the baptismal gown.

"This is going to be harder than I thought." He scowled. "I expected more."

"We have more than you do," I shot back, feeling defensive. "Do you think you can use Andora for the book?"

"We will discuss what I know downstairs."

Amelie was waiting in the living room with chai tea, pita chips, and hummus. Dr. Girard turned down the snack, but Colin dug in heartily. I didn't feel hungry, and chai gave me a stomachache. Between bites, Colin made notes in our casebook.

Dr. Girard sat on the edge of the couch and opened his briefcase. He pulled out a file. "I have a small housekeeping detail to take care of before we move forward. I spoke to my agent about the prospect of including Andora in my book. She faxed an agreement over this morning." He pulled a silver, expensive-looking pen from his shirt pocket. "Andi, since you're a minor and Amelie is your legal guardian, you'll both have to sign the form."

"What kind of agreement?" Amelie asked.

I sat beside him on the flowered sofa. He flipped through the form's pages and pointed to the line where I should sign. I'd never signed anything so official before. I didn't think the back of my library card counted.

"Hold on a minute," Amelie said. "Let me read that first."

Reluctantly, Dr. Girard handed Amelie the documents.

Mr. Rochester jumped onto the back of the couch

behind Dr. Girard. He cocked his head. I'd seen that same expression on his face before he pounced on his toy mouse. I reached behind me and moved the cat to my lap. Dr. Girard's lip curled and he scooted away from us. *Great, he doesn't like kids or animals.*

Amelie's eyes narrowed as they moved across the pages. "If I understand this correctly, you're asking for exclusive rights to this story. In other words, legally we can't give our consent to anyone else to write about it."

Dr. Girard sighed. "All due respect, Professor, but I don't think that's unreasonable."

"How long does this agreement last?"

He cleared his throat. "There is no set ending date."

Amelie's jaw tensed. "What if when Andi is an adult she wants to write about her experiences trying to uncover Andora's identity?"

"Really, is that very likely?" He looked at me and smiled. "What child would be interested in writing about history?"

"Andi might be, and I don't want to hold her back by signing something when she is only eleven years old and not ready to make that decision."

Dr. Girard's tone was hard now and he flushed. "I don't know what all the fuss is about. This is a standard agreement. As the author, I have rights to the story."

"And as relatives of Andora, we have rights to the story too. We need time to think this over. I'll have my lawyer take a look at it. And I'm sure we can come to an agreement by making some simple changes to the wording of this document."

"Amelie, I want—" I started to say that I just wanted to know about Andora. I didn't care about signing the paper.

Dr. Girard snatched the pages from Amelie's hand. "Really, Amelie. I've written two books and been published in dozens of journals. This is a standard agreement. I've never felt so insulted."

"That may be true," Amelie replied, her voice calm. "But you cannot object to me having my lawyer look it over. It is a legally binding document, isn't it?"

Dr. Girard stood abruptly. "This conversation is over. I don't need your permission to write about this mysterious relative of yours. I was doing you a favor by including you."

I jumped up. "But you haven't told us anything yet."

"Nor will I, under these circumstances. Andi, you have your aunt to thank for that."

"I think it's time for you to leave." Amelie's voice was cold.

Dr. Girard glowered. "Very well."

Colin jumped out of the armchair, sending pita chips tumbling to the floor. Mr. Rochester hissed at Dr. Girard with eyes wide and back arched.

The history professor glared at us all in turn, including Mr. Rochester, who hissed at him a second time. "Don't stand in my way," he warned. "There's a big story here, and I will get to the bottom of it with or without your help." He stomped out of the living room, yanked the front door open, and slammed it shut behind him.

When he was gone, I turned to my aunt. "How could you do that? He was going to tell us about Andora!"

Amelie's face fell. "Andi, I—"

"Now, we'll never know what happened to her."

"Andi, I had to protect you. That's my job."

"From what? A piece of paper? I don't care about that contract thing."

"You might not now, but you will someday. Let's ..."

Before she could finish her sentence, I stomped out of the room.

A day later, I sat at the picnic table in the backyard, reading over the casebook and stewing over Dr. Girard's words. Could he really steal Andora's story? Amelie told me he could write about Andora whether or not we signed the agreement. But she said it was good thing we didn't sign because her lawyer informed her that Dr. Girard's reaction sounded fishy. I still wished we'd signed it. Maybe then I'd know what Dr. Girard knows about Andora.

The telephone rang inside the house. Seconds later, Bethany poked her head out the back door. "It's for you. Some old guy."

Without thinking, I clenched my hands into fists, as if I were getting ready to punch someone. It was probably Dr. Girard calling to convince Amelie to sign the contract. When I didn't jump up and get the phone, Bethany placed it on a plastic chair by the back door. "You know, Andi, pouting won't finish cleaning out the attic or help you find Andora." She went back inside.

Said the Queen of the Pouters, I thought. I jumped off the picnic table and picked up the phone. "Hello?"

"Andi, it's Patrick Finnigan from the Historical Society."

"Oh hi, Mr. Finnigan," I said, my voice guarded. I remembered that he was the one who'd told Dr. Girard about our search for Andora.

"Amelie called and told me what happened yesterday," he said. "She wasn't very happy with me. And she had every right to be upset. I shouldn't have sent Dr. Girard to you."

"That's okay, Mr. Finnigan." I could imagine his black mustache drooping.

"No, it's not okay. I should have known he'd be more interested in getting the story than in helping you kids."

I held the phone up to my ear and waited.

"It's just that ... he's ... he's so well known. I thought that if Dr. Girard wrote a definitive work about Killdeer history, it would put our little museum and historical society on the map. With the right recognition, we'd have a better chance to get some grant money or even a few visitors."

I still didn't say anything. My mom and dad applied for tons of research grants to fund their botany lab. It always seemed like a lot of work to me.

"Anyway, I fully deserved Amelie's reprimands. Please allow me to make amends."

"Okay."

"Are you still interested in finding out more about Andora?"

"Yes!" I replied quickly.

Just then, Colin walked into the backyard and waved. I put my finger to my lips.

"Miss Addy is a good friend of mine," Mr. Finnigan said.

I sat up straighter and flashed Colin a thumbs-up. "Miss Addy?"

Colin sat next to me on the picnic bench and leaned in close to hear the other side of the conversation.

"I've interviewed her many times for the museum archives. In fact, I saw her just yesterday, and she told me that you'd asked her about Andora."

I held my breath. "You didn't tell Dr. Girard that, did you?"

"No. Thankfully, I kept that bit of information to myself." He spoke faster now, "I explained to Miss Addy why you're so interested in the name *Andora* and what you found in the attic. I hope that's okay." He paused. I heard the worry in his voice again.

"Yes, that's fine," I assured him. I wished he would get to the point. Colin looked prepared to grab the phone out of my hand. I scooted away from him just to be safe.

Mr. Finnigan chuckled. "You're lucky she detests Girard. When I told her what happened between the two of you, she was fit to be tied."

I held my breath.

"She has agreed to meet with you and asked me to

invite you to have tea at her home on Friday afternoon at four o'clock. I'll be there as well."

"And she'll answer any questions I have about Andora?"

"I think she will, Andi, but you have to let Miss Addy tell her story in her own time. She won't have it any other way. That's what got Dr. Girard in trouble. He wanted her to drive straight to the heart of the story. He wasn't interested in hearing about her impressions."

"Can Colin come too?"

Colin nodded so hard beside me, I thought his head would snap right off his neck.

"I thought you might ask that, and I've already arranged it with her. Be there early. Miss Addy doesn't tolerate lateness. She lives just a few blocks away from you. Colin knows where it is."

"Thanks, Mr. Finnigan."

"You're welcome. Again, I apologize for Dr. Girard's behavior."

"It's not your fault," I said, and this time I meant it.

As I carried an old baby stroller into the garage, I stopped in my tracks and gaped. Bethany was standing in the middle of the room, writing prices on stickers and placing them on items—everything from old Barbie dolls to window frames. But what really surprised me was the state of the stuff. All of the items were unpacked and organized by category in neat piles all around the garage. When the sale finally started at the end of the week, all we'd have to do is open the garage door and let the shoppers come inside.

I picked my jaw off the floor. "What happened in here?"

Bethany looked up from the coffee mugs she'd been pricing at twenty-five cents each. "What?"

"It's so neat and organized. You did this just today?"

She shrugged. "While you and Colin have been working up in the attic, I've been out here doing this. It's no big deal. Where is he anyway?"

"Still in the attic. I think we can start moving some of my stuff up there tomorrow."

"Good. Be sure to move that poster first."

I chewed my lip. "How is Zane?"

She glared at me. "That's none of your business."

"You haven't said anything about him since we moved here. I've been wondering what's going on."

"Just leave that baby stroller anywhere." Her face appeared pinched. "I have to go inside for a minute."

She ran out of the garage and almost knocked over Bergita who was on her way in. Bergita didn't try to stop Bethany. "She didn't look too happy," she said, placing a roll of price stickers on one of the long tables. "I brought her some more stickers."

I put the stroller in the front corner of the garage next to a pair of roller skates. "She's never happy."

"You might want to cut Bethany some slack. Moving here has been hard for her. It's a lot of change in a short period of time."

I frowned. "And it's been easy for me? I lost my parents too. I moved to a new place too."

"You did. But you're a different person and handle it differently. I think your sister has realized that you're tougher than she is."

"But I'm not." I tapped my toe against the wheel of the stroller. "And I wasn't our parents' favorite either. I heard her tell you that I was."

Bergita stuck her hands into her shorts pockets. "Eavesdropping?"

"Not on purpose."

"Ah, well, what your sister believes about how your parents felt is her issue, not yours. You need to give her time to work through it."

"In the meantime, she hates me," I said barely above a whisper.

"She doesn't hate you. She's jealous of you—and not just because of your parents."

I wanted to ask her what she meant by that, but she continued talking before I had the chance.

"Give her some time and space. But most of all, pray for her."

What Bergita didn't know was that I'd given up praying the day my parents died.

Over the next two days, I avoided my sister as much as possible while waiting anxiously for Friday, the day Colin and I were finally going to meet with Miss Addy. Colin and I spent most of that time in the attic. Once we'd finally cleared out everything I didn't want to keep, which was most of it, we had the dirty task of scrubbing the floorboards and walls. Because of his asthma, Colin had to take frequent breaks to get away from the smell.

Amelie took us to the hardware store to pick out some paint to replace the sailboat wallpaper. I settled on sky blue because it reminded me of the color of the Central American sky my father had talked so much about.

When taking breaks from the cleaning and painting, Colin and I read everything we could find at the public library and on the Internet about the 1930s and the Great Depression.

According to what we read, on December 16, 1929, which was the day Andora came into this world, the United States was in turmoil. The stock market had crashed in late October of that year, on a day that would be forever called Black Tuesday. Immediately after the Crash, people ran to their banks to withdraw all of their money. But for many, it was too late and they lost a fortune.

With no money to cover the payroll, businesses laid off workers by the hundreds. The worst of the layoffs came in 1933, but they started as early as late 1929 when Andora was born. Men and women woke up every morning well before sunrise to go out and look for work.

Even in rural areas like Killdeer, the Depression had a devastating effect. People could no longer afford to buy fresh fruits and vegetables, which meant the farmers' prices dropped dramatically. Acres of crops were left to rot in the fields and orchards because no one bought the produce.

Colin and I were sitting side by side on a paint-spattered tarp in the middle of the attic, as Colin read aloud to me from his iPad. Mr. Rochester sat at the edge of the tarp trying to flick blue paint from his paws. I'd told him to stay away from that paint tray.

"Listen to this," Colin said. "Children were the most severely harmed by the Crash. Many parents turned kids out of their homes because they could no longer feed their children. Some children found jobs in factories but worked in terrible conditions."

"Let me see."

He handed me the tablet computer, and I scrolled down through the article. "Here's something." I read aloud, "Sometimes parents sent their younger children to live in orphanages or with family members who weren't as severely impacted by the Depression."

"Do you think that's what happened to Andora?" Colin pushed his glasses up higher on his nose with his thumb.

"I hope Miss Addy can tell us."

When Amelie had said that Bergita organizes a two-day neighborhood garage sale every year, I'd pictured a few houses selling mismatched furniture and moth-eaten clothes. Boy, was I wrong. It was so much more than that. She got the entire street involved. Up and down Dunlap Avenue, neighbors scrounged their garages and basements for anything that might earn a buck. The neighborhood mothers rushed around their yards and yelled to their children to "get that dented flatware from under the buffet," "go find that broken synthesizer," and "bring out every empty hanger." Everyone hoped to make a profit off the out-of-towners who visited Killdeer during the university's annual Endless Summer Festival.

Bergita went so far as to ask the town council to close off our street to thru traffic on Friday and Saturday, and she even borrowed all of the church's eight-foot rectangular folding tables.

It was now early morning on the first day of the neighborhood garage sale. As Colin and I flipped over another table and set it upright on its legs in the middle of the street, I said, "Bergita doesn't mess around, does she?"

Colin grinned as he spread a yellow vinyl tablecloth over it and secured the table cover with masking tape. "No way. You should have seen her the year Killdeer celebrated its bicentennial—she was the committee chairperson. There was a parade that weekend, and the elephant rides were the best."

"Elephant rides?"

"Oh yeah," Colin said seriously. "Bergita borrowed the elephant from a friend who's an animal trainer."

Bethany rolled a wheeled cooler over to us and stopped. She put a hand on her hip. "Bergita wants the pop on this table." I noticed she wouldn't look me in the eye.

Colin looked from one sister to the other. Finally, he said, "Thanks. We can do it."

Bethany nodded and walked away.

"Is something wrong between you and Bethany?" He paused. "I mean, more than normal?"

I ignored his question. "Let's just unload this pop."

Colin opened the cooler without another word.

"Back up!" Bergita yelled. Colin's grandmother stood in the middle of the street, waving her hands in the air as she directed a food truck between two parked cars. The truck's hazard lights flashed on and off like angry red eyes, and the truck made a soft *beep-beep* sound as it backed into the space.

"Cut to the right!" she cried.

The back wheels shifted.

"Okay, keep coming back … a little more! A little more! There! Stop!"

The truck jerked to a stop. Bergita seemed pleased with the truck's placement and walked over to join Colin and me at the pop table. She wiped her hands on her shorts. "I do have to say that every year this event gets better and better. It's hard to top myself, but somehow I manage."

"Do many people from the festival come over to the sale?"

"It varies from year to year, but we'll have a good crowd. Don't you worry." She gestured up and down the street at the piles of sale items peppering the green lawns of Dunlap Avenue. "I know the type of people who go to the festival. They're mostly older alumni who like to go antique shopping on the weekends and love a good deal."

I watched as Amelie and Bethany helped a neighbor across the street set up a table filled with her kids' unwanted McDonald's Happy Meal Toys. "Do you have any antiques to sell?" I asked Bergita. "I mean, what makes something an antique, anyway?"

Colin said, "An antique is a collectible that's considered to have some type of value because of rarity, craftsmanship, the materials used, or a connection to a significant event. Typically, things that hold their value are considered 'antiques' if they're a hundred years old or more. Newer stuff is considered to be just collectibles."

Bergita shook her head at her grandson. "No more *Antiques Roadshow* for you."

At three o'clock I was moving a metal rack filled with old clothing from one end of our driveway to the other and back again. My mind drifted. What if Miss Addy didn't really know Andora? Where else could I look for her? I couldn't wait any longer to go to Miss Addy's house.

I found Colin emptying a box filled with old jelly jars. Each jar had a cartoon on the front of it: the Flintstones, Bugs Bunny, Mickey Mouse, and more. "I'm organizing them by parent company. See? Hanna-Barbera, Looney Tunes, and Disney."

"Are you ready to go?" I interrupted.

He looked at his watch. "It's only three o'clock."

I gave him a stern look. "Remember what Mr. Finnigan said. We shouldn't show up late."

He set aside his jelly jars. "Just let me grab the casebook."

"Hurry up," I said.

Colin ran inside his house. While I waited with my bike on the sidewalk, I noticed some of the neighbors were taking advantage of the current lull in potential customers. They headed inside their air-conditioned homes to escape the late afternoon heat and cool down. I kept looking back at Colin's front door. *What was taking him so long?*

When he finally reappeared, his hair stood on end and his T-shirt was askew. He had a notebook in his hand, but it wasn't the casebook.

"Where's the casebook?" I asked.

"I can't find it. Did you take it home last night?"

"No. I remember leaving it with you."

"Yeah, that's what I thought. But I can't find it anywhere. I hope it didn't get mixed in with the garage sale stuff."

"Where did you have it last?" I asked.

"I remember putting it in the middle of my desk this morning." Colin stuck the new green notebook and his football pencil in my backpack. He picked up his bike off the lawn and climbed onto the seat.

I glanced at my watch. It was now 3:45 p.m. "We'll look for it when we get back. We'd better leave now or we'll be late getting to Miss Addy's."

Miss Addy's house was a few blocks away from our neighborhood, but on the other side of the university. Colin led the way. We pedaled hard across campus, where many people busily finished preparing for the weekend's Endless Summer Festival, which would start later tonight. Tables and booths covered the campus grounds. In front of College Church, audio-visual geeks plugged in speakers and microphones on a newly constructed stage for Friday evening's symphonic band concert.

I hoped I could escape day two of the garage sale for an hour or so tomorrow—just to see what the festival is all about and maybe spread the word about the great sale happening on Dunlap Avenue.

Miss Addy's white house was shaped like a barn, and her yard was one huge flowerbed. The flower names came to me: impatiens, sweet woodruff, and bachelor's buttons. I bit my lip. My mother taught me those names. In the summer she would ask me to name the flowers we saw during walks around our old neighborhood. I was always eager to play this game with her. Bethany was not.

Behind me, I heard Colin trip on the bottom porch step at Miss Addy's. I screeched as I suddenly felt him grab a hold of my T-shirt and pull me down with him. Together we tumbled onto the steps in a heap.

"Ouch!" I yelped and pushed Colin off of me.

At that moment the front door opened and Miss Addy loomed above us. All four feet nine inches of her.

"I see you've found my home," she said, her voice hard like steel.

After Colin and I brushed the dirt off our clothes, Miss Addy led us into the house and invited us to sit on a tiny couch in the living room, which looked like it had been copied from some scene in a historical movie.

Mr. Finnigan was already sitting in an armchair that matched the couch.

Miss Addy disappeared into the kitchen to get the tea tray. I offered to help her, but Miss Addy shook her head with pursed lips. I suspected she thought I would trip and drop the tray.

After she'd left the room, Mr. Finnigan's head wagged back and forth between Colin and me. He chewed his lower lip. "What happened?"

I rubbed the side of my leg where Colin had bruised it with his elbow during the fall. "Colin tripped on the steps and fell on me."

Colin flushed red with embarrassment. "It was an accident."

"Did she see you?" Mr. Finnigan whispered.

"Yes," I whispered back.

"She won't—"

Just then, Miss Addy toddled back into the living room. "I won't what, Patrick?"

Mr. Finnigan grabbed a blueberry teacake from the tray and stuffed it into his mouth. Colin did the same.

Miss Addy looked at me and raised her thin eyebrows. I accepted the cup and saucer of tea from her and tried to smile the sweetest smile I could muster. I had mastered this kind of smile for those times when my parents hosted Science Department meetings at our house. Usually, our parents asked Bethany and me to make a brief appearance before our parents sent us to our rooms for the night.

One year I sat at the top of the stairs, listening to my parents laugh and talk with professors and students about the latest biological theories and research, and wishing I could join them. On those nights I longed to be more like Bethany who had no interest in science and could quietly go to her room and draw the night away. I, on the other hand, wanted to hear everything they had to say. I admit I didn't understand most of it. But I consoled myself by thinking that if I studied hard, then someday I might receive an invitation to one of my parents' gatherings when I was older. Now that would never happen.

"Andi, are you all right?" Miss Addy croaked.

My teacup almost slipped through my fingers. I

jerked it upright and spilled a hot drop of tea on my hand. "I'm fine."

Miss Addy handed Colin and Mr. Finnigan a teacup each, and then she sat down in an ancient-looking chair with wooden arms. She got right to the point.

"Patrick tells me you want to know what happened to Andora Boggs who was born in December of 1929. I have to say first off that I don't know anyone named Andora Boggs except for you."

I opened my mouth to speak. Mr. Finnigan shot me a glance, and I remembered his warning to let Miss Addy tell her story in her own way. I snapped my mouth shut.

Miss Addy took a sip of her tea and placed the teacup and saucer next to a ceramic figurine of a child playing the violin on the lace-covered coffee table.

"When you've lived as long as I have, the things that happened yesterday aren't as real to you as the things that happened decades ago." She threw us a beady look as if daring us to question her mental capabilities. "Many people today look back on the Great Depression with something like a fondness. And maybe I do too, a little. Maybe we feel that way because we made it through. But living through that time was difficult; and for some, it was unbearable."

Colin made notes in the green notebook. I hoped we'd be able to find the real casebook when we returned home.

"The last time I heard the name *Andora* was in 1933, and I was twelve years old." Miss Addy paused and slowly hoisted herself out of her chair, a tapestry-covered recliner with pieces of delicate lace pinned to the arms. She shuffled across the room to a roll top desk, lifted the wooden top, and removed something wrapped in brown paper. After she sat down again, she didn't say anything for a few excruciating seconds. I sat on my hands to stop myself from leaping out of my chair and grabbing the item from her hands.

On her lap she unwrapped a thin, red leather book with soft gray pages. She ran her wrinkled hands over it and said, "This is something very precious to me, which I will trust you to keep safe, Andi. Patrick tells me you are a bright and responsible young lady." She gave me a keen look, assessing my brightness and responsibility.

I felt my face burn, wondering what Miss Addy would think if she knew I'd just imagined ripping the book out of her frail arms. I hoped my most charming smile, which showed off my full set of braces, looked trustworthy.

"I'm encouraged that young people like you and Colin," she nodded toward him, "are interested in history. And your interest encouraged me to share this with you. I'm in my nineties, and it's high time I stopped holding on to things and started sharing them. I won't be around forever. Before long, my grandniece will pitch all of my belongings into boxes and send them off to the dump."

Mr. Finnigan shook his head. "Miss Addy, you have years ahead of you."

Miss Addy gave him a small smile. "That may be true, Patrick, but I no longer have decades ahead of me—nor do I want them. When it's time to go home to my great reward, I'll be ready."

She tapped the cover of the book with her fingernail. "When I was young, I fancied myself a writer. I wanted more than anything to write a great novel like *Gone with the Wind* or *The Grapes of Wrath*—both were bestsellers when I was a young woman. Lord knows nothing came of my desire. But at the advice of my English teacher, I kept a journal. I wrote in it quite a bit on the days that I couldn't go to school because I had to stay home and help Mother with the younger children. I thought of my journal as my schoolwork for the day. I desperately loved school."

She paused a moment and patted the journal on her lap. Her eyes had a dreamy look to them, and her voice was high and wistful when she continued, "In this journal I recorded my day-to-day activities. I hadn't read it in years. But after you-all stopped me after church on Sunday, I decided to dig it out and look for the answer as to why the name *Andora* startled me so much. And I found it."

My breath caught as Miss Addy carefully turned the delicate pages of the journal and nodded with satisfaction when she found the page she sought. In a sure, clear voice she read:

September 13, 1933

Ma gave me some bottles to return to the factory today. She said that Old Michael Pike would give me a penny for forty bottles. We found them yesterday in the Mill Street junkyard. Hard times there on Mill Street, Ma said.

I saw my friend Molly Fletcher picking through the junk heap with her family. Molly used to sit beside me in school, but she hasn't been there in a while. Her family lost their home. The landlord kicked them out because they couldn't pay their rent. I felt bad for taking the bottles from the junkyard-bottles that Molly could have collected and gotten a penny for. I knew she needed that penny more than I did. Maybe the money would help her come back to school. I dearly miss her on the playground. But Ma said we have to do everything we can to keep our family together now.

When I got to the factory, there was a long line of men dressed in their best Sunday clothes. They were all hoping to catch the foreman's eye. My Pa stood in that line many days, and then he came home with his head down low. Now he's gone north to Akron; he heard there is some work in the rubber factories up there. He'll send for us as soon as he can, Ma told me. But I'm not sure. I hear her crying at night.

I went around to the back of the factory where I was supposed to drop off the bottles. I knocked on the back door. The rough metal hurt my knuckles. As I waited, steam rolled from the two chimneys that poked out of the top of the factory.

The crate of bottles weighed heavy in my arms.

So I set it down in front of the door and knocked again. I heard somebody yelling behind me. I thought maybe it was the foreman or one of the workers. I thought maybe this person could tell me where to put the bottles and retrieve my penny. So I followed the sound around the building. Just before I rounded the corner, I heard someone cry out in dismay, "I've changed my mind! This isn't going to work."

"What do you mean? The deal's done. You have your fancy education and your money. It's been three years."

I peeked around the corner and saw Michael Pike III standing with a worker dressed in denim overalls. The man in the overalls was Mr. Boggs. I recognized him because he and his wife go to my church.

"My wife," Mr. Boggs began, dabbing the sweat from his forehead with a stained handkerchief, "she's having trouble this time. If Emily could just see her, it would be such a comfort."

Mrs. Emily Boggs is pregnant with her second child. She lost her first baby a few winters back. I remember Ma telling me never to mention it because it was still a painful subject for them. The infant died suddenly, heartrendingly.

"We're all having a hard time now," Mr. Pike said in a cold voice.

But Mr. Boggs didn't let it go. He tucked his handkerchief back inside his front pocket and folded his hands together, pleading. "Just for the afternoon, that's all I ask. Emily is still mourning Andora—"

Mr. Pike towered above Mr. Boggs, his face red with fury. "Don't mention that name!" Mr. Pike hissed. "Don't ever mention that name!"

Mr. Boggs stepped back and bowed his head. "I'm sorry, sir."

"Now get back on the line, or one of the hundreds of men lined up out front will do it for you."

Mr. Boggs nodded and turned away. I didn't want the men to see me watching them, so I ran around the side of the building. Forgetting about my crate full of bottles, I ran all the way home. When I got there, Ma asked me for the penny. I told her I didn't have it; I'd lost it on the way. She walloped me good for that.

My head spun as Miss Addy closed her journal. My heart ached with the pain of a lost friend—a friend I thought of almost all the time now, even though I never knew her. Andora was dead.

I shook my head and tried to sort out my thoughts. The proof was right there in Miss Addy's journal. Great-Grandma Emily lost her first child. But then, why haven't we found any mention of Andora's death in the archives? Maybe the obituary is still there, but we didn't search long enough for it. After I found Andora's birth announcement, we stopped looking through the newspapers. We shouldn't have stopped.

I glanced at Mr. Finnigan and waited for permission to speak. He nodded. I swallowed. "Miss Addy, are you saying Andora died?" I needed to hear it spoken out loud, to know for certain.

"I'm afraid that's what happened, child."

Another person I'd grown to love, gone.

I squeezed my eyes shut. Then I bit my lip and opened my eyes again. "So searching for her was a big waste of time?"

I could feel Colin's eyes on me. But I couldn't look back at him, not yet. My voice broke as I said, "Why didn't the newspaper mention her death?"

Miss Addy shook her head.

Mr. Finnigan jumped into the conversation. "Maybe the family asked the newspaper to leave it out. Everyone in town would have known already."

"It could still be there," Colin piped up, echoing my thoughts. "We just need to keep looking. Do you know when Andora died, Miss Addy?"

She opened her journal again and flipped through the pages. "Well, based on this entry, it sounds like it happened around the winter of 1930."

"She died as a baby." My fingers balled into a tight fist. I tried to relax my hand, and my knuckles cracked.

Miss Addy leaned toward me and took my hand in hers. "I'm starting to remember Mr. and Mrs. Boggs a little better. Andi, let me assure you that your Great-Grandfather Patterson was crushed when Andora died. Truly crushed. But his heartache was nothing compared to that of Emily's. Mothers and daughters always have a special bond between them, and Emily lost her chance to have that bond with her baby girl."

I thought of my own mother. I pictured her chipped fingernails caked with mud from digging in the compost pile in our backyard, and her secret wink meant just for me. I pushed the memory of Mom away before she could overcome me, and I concentrated on Andora. Andora. Baby Andora. Dead.

"Your great-grandmother fell into a state of denial. Everyone copes with death in a different way," Miss Addy said, not knowing that she was repeating what I'd overheard Bergita saying to Bethany earlier that week. "Some people said she forgot the child ever existed or that the baby ever lived with her." Miss Addy's black eyes, now soft with compassion, made her look so different than that stern, tiny woman I'd met at church.

"But," I protested with a soft breath. "But ..."

"Patterson didn't want to cause Emily more pain, so he asked the town not to speak of Andora anymore. To act as if the child had never lived."

Miss Addy's voice was gentle and she lightly squeezed my hand, but her words still felt like a slap.

"The whole town loved Emily, so they all agreed. That's why in my journal I wrote that Ma asked me not to mention it to the Boggs. I imagine that's why Patterson hid Andora's things in that little cubby in your attic, Andi. He couldn't bear to part with them, but he didn't want Emily to be reminded of the daughter she never had an opportunity to know."

"And that explains why I couldn't find an obituary," Mr. Finnigan added.

I looked at him. "You've been searching for it?"

He nodded, looking sheepish. "I've searched ever since you kids asked me about her. I thought I could surprise you with a lead, but I came up with nothing."

"That solves the case then." Colin sounded disappointed.

I'd finished my mission. I now knew who Andora was and what had happened to her. Yet I felt no satisfaction. Andora's mystery had helped me to regain a sense of control over my life—something I hadn't felt since my parents died. I didn't want to let it go. I didn't want to let Andora go.

"But after Emily died, why didn't Patterson say anything?" I asked. "Why didn't he tell my grandpa that he'd had a sister?"

"Maybe he did but your grandfather decided not to tell anyone," Colin said.

"Why wouldn't he tell anyone after his parents were gone?" I snapped.

Colin winced, but I was too distraught to feel sorry about lashing out at him.

"Maybe it was too painful for him too," Miss Addy said.

I stared down at my sneakers, thinking hard and

trying harder not to cry. What did my great-grand-father fight about with Michael Pike III? What did it have to do with money? And why couldn't Patterson mention the name *Andora* to Michael Pike III? Something didn't fit.

"Andora's death doesn't solve everything," I said. "Miss Addy, do you know what Michael Pike III was referring to when he said, 'You have your fancy education and your money'?"

She shook her head. "No. Men argued over money quite a lot in those days. I suppose they still do. But during the Depression, everyone was so hard up that money literally equaled life or death to a family."

"I think it means Michael Pike III paid Patterson for something, and I think it was for something more than working in the factory," Colin interjected.

After some thought, Mr. Finnigan spoke up. "It almost sounds like Michael Pike paid for Patterson's education at the university."

"But why would he do that? Miss Addy, would you please read that line again—the one about the money?"

Quietly, she found the page. "Here it is. Mr. Pike said, 'What do you mean? The deal's done. You have your fancy education and your money. It's been three years.'"

I thought hard. Colin and Mr. Finnigan were right. It sounded like Michael Pike III had paid Patterson for something.

Miss Addy sighed heavily, as if the memory of the Great Depression clung to her still.

Mr. Finnigan glanced at the mantel clock above the fireplace. "It's time for us to go, kids."

But I had more questions. Where was Andora buried? Did Miss Addy remember the funeral? I opened my mouth to ask, and then I saw how drawn and tired she looked. I held my tongue.

"Can we come again?" Colin asked.

She gave Colin a worn smile. "Of course you can. Thank you for coming to see me today. But I think I need to rest now." She squeezed my hand with surprising strength. And then she wrapped the brown paper around her journal once again and placed it in my lap. "Honey, take this. It might help you find what you're looking for." She made a face. "Although, you'll have to forgive me for the fragmented thoughts. They're just childhood ramblings."

She released my hand at last, and I held the worn journal to my chest. "Thank you, Miss Addy." I managed a smile.

Mr. Finnigan watched me slip the journal into my backpack next to the substitute casebook. He chewed his lower lip but didn't say anything. Maybe he was worried that I wouldn't take good care of it.

I now wished that I'd brought the little blue trunk, the china doll, and the wooden blocks along. Miss Addy would probably like to see them. Next time I visited her, I'd bring them.

Miss Addy insisted on walking us to the door to say good-bye. I hugged my backpack to my chest.

"I'll take good care of it, I promise," I told her.

She patted my shoulder with her wrinkled hand. Her other hand had a firm grip on her cane.

Mr. Finnigan said good-bye to us. Colin and I picked up our bikes from the plush green lawn, and Mr. Finnigan walked down the street to his car parked on the opposite side of Miss Addy's house. Colin jumped on his bike, but I just stood beside mine and watched Mr. Finnigan for a moment.

"Come on," Colin said. "We have to get back to the garage sale now or Bergita will have a fit."

"Right." I straddled my bike and watched Mr. Finnigan drive away.

Colin waited in the middle of the street. "Are you coming?" he asked.

I put my feet on the bike pedals. "We have to make a stop first."

Colin rode his bike alongside mine. "Where are we going?"

"The university library. If Number Three paid for my great-grandfather to go to college, then maybe they have a record of it in their archives."

"That's a great idea, Andi!" Colin pedaled faster.

The library was an enormous building with huge white pillars in front. Colin and I left our bikes at the side of the building and ran up the steps to the front door. Even though it was just an hour since we'd rode through campus, the place now seemed deserted. The Endless Summer Festival would begin at 6:00 p.m. that night.

I yanked the door handle. It didn't budge.

"It's closed." Colin squinted at a nearby sign. "This sign says it closes at 4:30 p.m. on Fridays during the summer. We just missed it." He frowned. "And because of the festival, it's closed all weekend and won't reopen again until Monday morning at 9 a.m."

My shoulders drooped. I was certain there'd be another clue about Andora in the library.

"Maybe Amelie can talk to the librarian on Monday and find out about Patterson's tuition?" Colin suggested.

"That's three days from now," I said. My gaze wandered across the grounds. The university library stood across The Green from Whit Hall, where Dr. Girard's office was located.

Suddenly the door to Whit Hall opened, and Dr. Girard stepped outside. I grabbed Colin's arm.

"Get down!" I hissed, pulling him behind the library's metal book drop.

Colin tried to peek around the side of the container. "What is it?"

"Dr. Girard. He just came out of Whit." I slowly poked my head out. Not seeing anyone, I stood up. "I think he's gone."

Colin followed me down the library steps. "Why did we hide from him?"

"He's still upset that Amelie wouldn't sign that contract, and I don't want him to try talking me into it right now." I frowned. "He's really set on writing that book. When I was in his office on Sunday, I heard him talking to his agent on the phone. He said he'd write a proposal for her by the end ... " My mouth fell open.

Colin stared at me. "What? What is it?"

"The proposal. If we could see it, then we'd know what Dr. Girard is planning to do with Andora's story."

My pulse quickened. "When Dr. Girard's secretary showed up on Sunday, he asked her to finish working on the book proposal before she leaves on vacation—today. It has to be the same proposal. And maybe it's sitting on her desk right now."

Colin adjusted his glass. "Are you suggesting what I think you are?"

I nodded. "We have to get inside that office."

Colin was a few paces behind me as I crept around Whit Hall to the window of the workroom in the History Department.

"Andi," he whispered, "maybe we shouldn't be doing this?"

"Let's just see if the window is still unlocked. If it's locked, we'll head straight home."

I removed the screen and pushed up on the window. It silently slid open.

"Now what do we do?" Colin asked.

I bit my lip. "I think that means we go in."

Colin hesitated. "That's breaking and entering."

"Technically ... but how else are we going to see the proposal?" I took off my backpack. "Hold this. You stay here and keep watch. I'm going in."

"Andi ..."

I hoisted myself onto the windowsill. I got only as far as my stomach and then dangled there. "Give me a boost."

Colin sighed and pushed the bottoms of my sneakers. I pulled myself the rest of the way inside by holding on to the edge of the worktable below the window. I slid across the tabletop and sent a pair of scissors and a stapler flying. As I hit the floor of the workroom, I froze and waited to hear if anyone had heard all of the noise I'd just made.

The rest of the office was silent.

I stuck my head out the window and whispered, "All clear."

"Hurry up."

"Okay." I pulled my head back inside the room. The door to the workroom was closed. Slowly, I opened it. The hallway and the outer office were dark. I headed straight for the secretary's desk. There was just enough light streaming in from the window to see that her desktop was clear. Not that I expected the proposal to be sitting on her keyboard, but it would have been nice. I opened a few drawers and found a stash of candy that would give any dentist a heart attack and an amazing number of stress balls. No proposal.

On the wall across from her desk were mailboxes for all of the professors in the department. Dr. Girard's box was empty, but there was a thick manila envelope lying in the out-box.

"Andi!" Colin called, his voice muffled by the distance. "Hurry up!"

I carefully opened the envelope and pulled out the first page. BOOK PROPOSAL it said across the top. I'd found it. I took the envelope back to the secretary's desk and pulled out all of the sheets of paper. The proposed title of the book was "Little Girl Lost."

I flipped through the pages, scanning for Andora's name. I found it on the fourth page. "Andora Boggs was a poor girl born in a time of poverty—"

"Andi!" Colin's cry sounded more desperate.

I hurried back to the workroom. "What is it?"

"Andi, we need to leave. Someone could come. And I have no good reason to be lurking outside this open window on a Friday evening."

I pointed to the page. "This is where he talks about Andora."

"Andi ... "

"Okay, okay. Let me make a copy of it." I turned on the copy machine, and hit the Copy button. After the copier was finished, I returned the original page about Andora to where it belonged in the stack of pages, put everything back inside the manila envelope, and ran the envelope to the outbox in the outer office.

Back in the workroom, I folded my photocopy and stuck it in my shorts pocket before climbing onto the worktable. I stuck my feet out the window and got ready to jump down.

"Hey, what are you doing?" a gruff voice shouted as I hit the ground. Colin helped me to my feet as a university security guard ran toward us.

The security guard then made us walk our bikes to his office in the guardhouse near the main entrance of campus. We waited there for Amelie to pick us up. At least I'd managed to convince him to call Amelie instead of the police.

Amelie stomped into the guardhouse fifteen minutes later. "Andora Boggs, I can't believe you broke into a building!"

"I caught her red-handed," the security guard said.

"Thank you, Wally. And thank you for not filing a report."

He smiled at her and scowled at Colin and me. "You're lucky your aunt is such a nice lady, or you'd be at the police station right now facing charges for criminal trespass."

Amelie wrapped an arm around Colin's and my shoulders. "Load your bikes into the back of my Jeep. We're going home."

Amelie was silent during the drive back to Dunlap Avenue.

Colin and I sat perfectly still in the backseat.

Amelie parked the Jeep in the driveway. Colin got out and removed the bikes from the back. I went to help him. My aunt folded her arms. "Colin, it's time for you to go home." She didn't have to ask him twice. He waved at me and ran his bike across the yard.

Bethany stood on the front porch with her arms wrapped around her waist, watching us.

Amelie closed her eyes for a moment. "You've taken this Andora thing too far. You can't break into someone's office. And this is the second time you've done it in a week! What if Dr. Girard found out?"

I dropped my head. "I'm sorry, Amelie."

"You're grounded, too. Tomorrow is the second day of the neighborhood garage sale, and you can help with that because you made a commitment. But for the next week, you're not going anywhere else."

I opened my mouth to protest.

"Don't argue with me. I see I've let you girls think I'm just your pal, but I'm your parent now. Like it or not, I'm going to start acting like it. Now go inside."

I ran up the steps, past my sister, and into the house.

That night was my first night sleeping in my attic bedroom. It would have been a happier occasion if I didn't feel so terrible about being grounded. I sat in the middle of my bed with Mr. Rochester purring in my lap. I read and re-read the page that I'd copied from Dr. Girard's book proposal. It didn't tell me anything I didn't already know, except for the last line: "Andora Boggs is still alive." I stared at it.

If Andora didn't die, then what happened to her?

The ladder leading up to my room creaked, and Bethany's head appeared in the opening.

I stuck the sheet of paper under my pillow.

"Hey," Bethany said.

I stroked Mr. Rochester's back. "Hey."

"So, you're grounded." Bethany smiled. "It's your first time. How does it feel?"

"Crummy."

"Well as someone who's had a lot of grounding experience, I say enjoy it. It's not that bad, and I bet it will give you a lot of time to read more about the Great Depression."

I grunted.

"It's kind of nice to have you get in trouble for once. Mom and Dad were always grounding me, but they never grounded you. You were their perfect child."

"No, I wasn't."

She shrugged as if it didn't matter. "You were." She crossed the room and sat on my desk chair. Mr. Rochester jumped off my lap and ran to hers.

I was going to argue with her some more but then she changed the subject, "Zane's not talking to me anymore. That's why I got mad when you asked about him."

"Why not?"

She ran her fingers through Mr. Rochester's fur. "He said it's too hard to keep a friendship, or whatever we had, with me being so far away. I've texted him a bunch of times, but he hasn't texted back." She bit her lip. "Now I'm like one of those desperate girls who's been dumped."

I turned and set my feet on the floor. "It's his loss. He was always a jerk, if you ask me."

Bethany blinked away tears. "He was nice to me after Mom and Dad died."

I paused then said, "I miss Mom and Dad too."

She frowned. "I know that."

"You do?" I raised an eyebrow.

"You don't think I do?"

I twisted my mouth. "I heard you tell Bergita that I don't miss them." She glowered at me, but I continued anyway. "And I wasn't their favorite child either. How many times did I have to hear them rave about your art?"

"Maybe."

"You didn't feel the same pressure that I felt with Mom and Dad. I was always trying to be like them. You never worried about that."

She watched me for a moment. "I guess I never thought of it that way." She stood and Mr. Rochester jumped to the floor. "I just wanted to say I'm glad you're home and I'm glad I didn't have to use my portion of the garage sale money to bail you out of jail."

"Thanks."

She started down the ladder and then stopped with her head and shoulders still inside the room. "I love the attic room, by the way. It's really cool." She pointed at the periodic table poster hanging over my desk. "And that looks good there."

"Thanks." I swallowed. "And thanks for your help with the garage sale."

She shrugged. "I got my texting back. Zane's not the only person in the world that I can text." She climbed the rest of the way down.

I woke up in the attic with Mr. Rochester asleep on my head. I stretched and knocked my patchwork quilt to the floor. For the first time since the move, I didn't have that uneasy feeling of waking up in an unfamiliar place. The attic had become my bedroom. Amelie's house had become my home.

And then I remembered that I was grounded.

I reached over to my nightstand and picked up the little elephant block that I kept there. I stared at it and thought about what I'd learned from Miss Addy yesterday and our adventure on campus.

I jumped off the bed, walked over to my desk, and pulled open the middle drawer. Most of my things were still down in Bethany's room, so only Miss Addy's journal was in there.

I flipped through the pages. The red leather was so

soft that it felt like cloth. The onionskin pages were a light gray, and some of them clung together. I separated them as gently as I could. The events in the journal spanned from January to December 1933, just one year in the life of a Killdeer girl. I could hardly wait to read it.

"Andi! Are you up?" Amelie's groggy voice floated through the hatch.

"Yeah," I called back.

"Well, get down here!"

The journal would have to wait. I returned it to my desk and shut the drawer.

I looked down the ladder at Amelie who was still wearing her pajamas. Her long hair was up in a messy knot on top of her head like a sumo wrestler. She yawned. "Good, you're awake. You take the first shift today." She rubbed her eyes. "My word, it's way too early."

I gave a sigh of relief that she didn't say anything more about last night.

Ten minutes later, I ran outside and gasped. It was only eight in the morning, and police officers were adjusting barricades on either end of the road to stop the traffic. Food vendors in white trailers sold Indian fry bread, sausage sandwiches, and cotton candy. Homeowners up and down the street made final touches to their displays. The sale would officially start at nine, but customers were already wandering up and down the street.

I grabbed a muffin and a cup of lemonade from a free breakfast table that Bergita had set up in her front yard. And then I headed to our garage. Amelie had already opened the door for me. I had until noon to convince people to buy things they didn't really need. Then Amelie would take over.

I pulled an old dress form out onto the driveway as Amelie stumbled out of the house and started walking toward campus for the Endless Summer Festival. She would be sitting at the literary magazine table this morning. Bethany, dressed for a fashion shoot in a mini skirt and flowered top, followed her. Her art class instructor had invited Bethany to sit at the Art Department's table with some of her work on display.

After they were gone, I sat on a lawn chair in the driveway, surrounded by decades of my family's possessions. Even though they didn't really belong to me, a part of me felt funny seeing them go. They'd been my constant companions over the last couple of weeks. I'd discovered them in unmarked boxes, sorted them, cleaned them, helped Bethany price them, and now I watched them drive away in the back of a minivan or the bed of a pickup truck.

Colin waved from his yard where he was helping Bergita add some last-minute touches to their display. Jackson surveyed their progress from the porch. Their setup really was impressive.

Colin ran over to me, waving the casebook. "I found it."

I gave a sigh of relief. "Thank goodness. Where was it?"

He blushed. "Under my bed." He handed it to me. "You keep it from now on. Is Amelie still mad?"

"She seemed better this morning, but I'm grounded."

Colin grimaced. "Sorry."

"What about you?"

He shrugged. "Nothing. I don't think Amelie told Bergita what happened."

I held the casebook to my chest. "I guess that's good news."

Colin opened his mouth as if to say something more, but Bergita yelled, "Colin, get over here and help me move these bowling balls!"

By ten o'clock, I'd sold a chest of drawers, two boxes of wire hangers, three football trophies, and a life-sized stuffed unicorn. I folded the five-dollar bill from my last sale and slipped it into the hot pink fanny pack I was using as a money belt. I spotted Mr. Finnigan thumbing through our collection of record albums. I zipped the fanny pack closed and walked up behind him. "Looking for something to add to the museum?"

Mr. Finnigan jumped.

"I'm sorry, Mr. Finnigan. I didn't mean to scare you."

He patted his chest. "I'm all right." He pulled a white handkerchief out of his back pants pocket and dabbed his sweaty forehead.

"Can I help you find something?"

"No, no, just looking. Amelie mentioned the garage sale to me. So I came by to see it for myself." He looked from the yards littered with wares to the food vendors parked in the middle of the street. "I must say, your aunt didn't exaggerate."

I grinned. An elderly couple approached the garage

and looked at a box of broken china with interest. I started to walk toward them.

Mr. Finnigan coughed. "Excuse me, Andi. Do you still have Miss Addy's journal?"

Distracted, I looked back toward the couple who was now drifting away from the broken china. If I didn't grab them now, I would lose the sale. "Yes."

"And it's safe?"

I made a face. "Sure. It's up in my room."

He smiled at me. "Good, good. It's so important to Miss Addy. I'd hate for it to get lost."

"I won't lose it," I said firmly, still watching the couple out of the corner of my eye.

"Of course, you won't." He dabbed his forehead again. "Well, I must be off. The museum is open today. I'm expecting some visitors from the festival to drop by."

I nodded and hurried over to the elderly couple. "Three dollars for the whole box," I said.

That got their attention.

Amelie settled into the lawn chair on the driveway promptly at noon. I handed her the fanny pack, and she opened it with surprise. "You made a killing! Are you sure you want to be a scientist and not a business mogul?"

"I even sold the broken china," I said proudly.

She grinned. "Not bad for someone who's grounded."

I relaxed. She wasn't mad anymore.

I ran into the house and up the ladder into my attic

room. Even if I was grounded, I could still read Miss Addy's journal. And Mr. Finnigan's question had made me nervous about it. I pulled open the middle desk drawer.

The journal was gone.

How could the journal be gone? I saw it just that morning.

Colin pulled his head out from under my bed and sneezed. He wasn't wearing his surgical mask, and his eyes were red and puffy. Even with all of the junk now removed to the garage, an army of dust bunnies still camped out in the attic. "Are you sure that's where you put it? Remember, I thought I lost the casebook yesterday. But it was just in a different place."

"We've looked everywhere a thousand times. It's not here!"

"You didn't take it out of the house?" he asked me for the four-hundredth time.

"I already told you I didn't." I sat on my desk chair. "I can't believe it's gone." I felt sick to my stomach remembering how Miss Addy had trusted me with her precious journal, a journal that had survived for eighty years until I'd gotten a hold of it. "We have to tell Mr. Finnigan," I said. "We should go right now."

"Andi, you're grounded. I had to sneak in the house just to help you look for it," Colin argued.

"I know. But it's Miss Addy's journal. We'll be back before Amelie even knows we're gone."

Colin's bangs fell over his glasses and he pushed them aside. "Okay. Mr. Finnigan knows Miss Addy better than we do. He'll know how to tell her."

Thankfully, when Colin and I went to collect our bikes, Amelie was distracted by a buyer who was interested in buying that old dress form. As they haggled over the price, Colin and I made a clean getaway.

We parked our bikes outside the museum door, which was unlocked. Although the building was open for visitors, Mr. Finnigan was nowhere in sight.

Colin coughed. "Well, I guess you lucked out. He isn't here."

I picked up a brochure sitting on Mr. Finnigan's desk. "The door's unlocked. He has to be here." I glanced around the reception area and saw that Mr. Finnigan had placed a coffee urn and some paper cups on a small card table in one corner. A little sign beside the urn read, WELCOME, GUESTS!

I glanced in the trash can beside the table. Empty. Poor Mr. Finnigan. He hadn't had any visitors.

"Let's look for him." I wanted to get my confession over with as soon as possible. I thought it best to treat this situation like ripping off a Band-Aid: Do it fast. "He's probably in the archives."

Our footsteps echoed on the stone floor as we walked past the gallery of photographs depicting Michael Pike Ginger Ale executives sitting behind their wide cherry desks, and employees polishing bottles on the factory floor.

We were still a ways down the hall from the archives, when I paused in front of the four portraits of the Pike family—all of the Michael Pikes and Margaret. I stared at Margaret's portrait and noticed again how she looked nothing like her dark-haired, olive-skinned relatives. And then my brain clicked.

"Andi," Colin whispered.

I waved him away as I thought about this some more. Dr. Girard's book proposal claimed that Andora didn't die as a baby. Miss Addy wrote that Patterson had asked Number Three if Emily could see "her" because Emily was sad. What if Margaret was Andora? What if my great-grandfather had given Andora to the Pikes so he could attend college? I felt sick to my stomach. Could I be right?

I didn't have time to tell Colin my theory because shouts erupted from further down the hall. I pressed my finger to my lips as Colin and I silently slid along the wall toward the open door.

After a few moments, I determined that the shouts were actually yelps of joy. "This is it! My golden ticket! This book is going to change everything!"

I stood as close to the doorframe as I dared, and instantly recognized a second voice: Mr. Finnigan.

"And you will give credit to the historical society and the museum?"

"Yes, yes," the first voice snapped.

Colin gasped beside me as we both recognized the first voice.

"Dr. Girard," Colin whispered.

I clamped my hand over his mouth and we froze.

"I still think we should tell the family and explain to them—"

"I'm not going to waste my time on that family," Dr. Girard said. "I have an agent and now an editor breathing down my neck. They wanted this book a year ago. Now I have all the evidence I need to make it happen."

"But what about Miss Addy?"

"What about her? That crazy old bat probably doesn't even remember giving the journal to the girl."

I balled my hands into fists at my sides, and I felt my face grow hot. I wouldn't be a bit surprised if my ears released some steam. I looked at Colin in the dim light of the hallway. Shock and disappointment washed across his face. And even though we'd only known each other for a short while, I knew his shock wasn't due to the history professor's words.

I had known I couldn't trust Dr. Girard the moment I first met him. I had a gut feeling about him. But my gut feeling about Mr. Finnigan had turned out to be wrong. By the look on Colin's face, I knew he felt the same betrayal I did. I thought Mr. Finnigan was our friend and Miss Addy's friend. I thought he cared about Andora and what had happened to her.

Furious, I stomped right into the archive room. Colin trailed behind me. The two men's eyes widened. Both of their mouths formed small Os just like those Honey Nut Cheerios Amelie had given to me on my first morning in Killdeer. Their facial expressions might have made me laugh out loud if I hadn't been so steaming mad.

Dr. Girard held Miss Addy's journal in his hand. My eyes trained on it. He gathered himself up like a proud peacock, ready for anything. "Andi! How nice to see you. Are you here to do more research?"

"I'm here for that journal," I said through clenched teeth, holding out my hand. "Give it to me. Now." I didn't really think he would respond to a direct order, but it was worth a shot.

Dr. Girard laughed, wrapped the journal in its brown paper cover, and slipped it into an open briefcase on the desk.

"Missy Addy trusted me with it. Give it back." I didn't drop my hand but continued to hold it out, palm up, expectant and stubborn.

He closed and latched the briefcase, and then stood it up on the desk beside him. He rolled his eyes. "Nice try, kid, but I need this journal much more than you do."

"Andi, I ... Dr. Girard asked to see the journal. To borrow it. He has every intention of returning it to Miss Addy someday," Mr. Finnigan stammered.

"Of course I do," Dr. Girard said smoothly.

I whipped my head around to face Mr. Finnigan. "You stole it from my house."

"I ... I ..."

"You asked me where I kept the journal. I thought you were concerned about it for Miss Addy's sake. But you stole it!" I cried, feeling the full impact of his betrayal for the first time. "If I'd known you wanted to steal it for *him*, I never would have told you where it was."

"Come, come," Dr. Girard said. "You're getting yourself all worked up over nothing."

"Miss Addy trusted *me* with it, not you."

"That journal isn't the only source of information. Look around you." He waved his arms around the room.

Colin slowly stepped out from behind me and inched his way toward the briefcase while the two men were focused on me. *Distract them,* I thought to myself.

The history professor smirked. "I suspected for years that something wasn't quite right about the Michael Pike family tree. And now I know what it was: Boggs genes."

"I already know that Margaret Pike is Andora."

Colin gaped at me, but I concentrated on Dr. Girard.

The history professor's lips curved into a smile. "Ahh, so you're really as smart as everyone claims. Bravo! But do you know the whole story?" He waited for me to answer. When I said nothing, he said, "I didn't think so. Well, let me tell you a little story then." He was thoroughly enjoying his own performance. "It's a story about a little girl who was sold to the highest bidder."

A sinking feeling settled over me.

"Mrs. Emily Boggs, a healthy country girl, and Mrs. Beatrice Pike, wife of Michael Pike III, were pregnant at the same time. Emily had her baby in mid-December of 1929. This was shortly after the terrible Stock Market Crash, so little Andora was born into a chaotic world and to a poor family. Her father, Patterson, worked at the bottling company just like every other man living in Killdeer at that time. He worked on the floor as a mechanic, but he dreamed of something bigger. He and Emily had moved to Killdeer from the mountains of West Virginia because Patterson had dreams of attending Michael Pike College. After the Crash, it looked like those dreams were over. Every day another coworker was laid off, and long lines of men looking for work formed outside the bottling company every morning. Patterson was replaceable, and he knew it."

My heartbeat quickened. "But my great-grandfather *did* go to Michael Pike College. He graduated and then became a professor. He taught there for years. He even has a building named after him. It's a small one, but how many people can say that?"

A malicious grin slid across Dr. Girard's face as he continued his story. "Beatrice didn't have a strong constitution like Emily did. From the beginning, her pregnancy was troubled. The doctor put her on bed rest for the last three months. And even though her baby wasn't due until late February, the local paper announced the birth of Margaret "Peggy" Pike on February second. Beatrice's baby was born premature.

"Late in March, Andora Boggs died of a mysterious

illness, and no one knew what caused it. The casket remained closed at the funeral. And you would have known all of that by now if you'd thought to check the records at College Church. Churches record all kinds of helpful information: baptisms, confirmations, and funerals," he smirked.

"But back to my story. A month after Andora's death, Beatrice and her daughter, whom everyone thought would die in infancy, made their first public appearance. Coincidental, don't you think? The girl was a beautiful child with fair skin and a full head of *red* hair. Strange that neither of her parents had red hair, wouldn't you say?

"Sadly, Emily never recovered from her daughter's death, and she died after giving birth to her son Brighton in November 1933. Those are the facts that are known. And your little adventure these last few days confirmed the rest of my suspicions. Thank you for that." He gave me an oily smile, and I fought the urge to slap him.

"Although most of the employees at the factory were laid off or replaced for lower-paid workers, Patterson never lost his job. In fact, he was given a raise after the death of his daughter. And then in the fall of 1930, he enrolled in classes at Michael Pike College. I made some inquiries in the university archives, and you'd never guess who paid for your great-grandfather's education."

He waited for my answer, but I refused to give him the satisfaction.

"Michael Pike III. Now *that* piqued my interest,

so I started digging further. After all, nobody ever praised Michael Pike III for his generosity toward his employees.

"The conversation that Miss Addy overheard as a child is just the evidence I need to make my suspicions public. Your great-grandfather sold Andora to the Pike family for job security and a college education."

It's what I'd already suspected, what I already knew, but that didn't make it any easier to hear—to know that someone I was related to could sell their own child. "What about Beatrice's daughter—the baby that was born premature?"

"It was common knowledge that Beatrice had suffered a miscarriage before. I suspect that's what happened to the real Peggy."

"But ..."

"The Pikes were desperate for a child—an heir to the family fortune," Dr. Girard said smugly. Then he walked over to Mr. Finnigan and clamped a hand on his shoulder, carelessly abandoning the briefcase on the desk. "I shared my suspicions with Patrick here, and he helped me with the research."

I turned on Mr. Finnigan then. "You knew! When Colin and I came here asking about Andora that first time, you already knew about her."

"I'm sorry, Andi. But can't you see that the museum isn't doing well?" He waved his arms around the room. "There are hundreds of people in town today for the festival, and not one of them has stopped by the museum. They'd rather go to your neighborhood garage sale than come here. If we had the notoriety ..." Mr. Finnigan trailed off.

I glared at him. I was so angry that I couldn't speak.

Colin moved faster than I imagined possible as he grabbed the briefcase off the desk. "Run!" Colin yelled, slipping through the doorway and running down the hall. I was right behind him.

I heard Dr. Girard yelling behind us, "We have to stop them! That briefcase has all of my research in it!"

I didn't look back.

"Outside to the bikes!" I shouted to Colin as we thundered down the hallway, the pounding feet of a furious Dr. Girard hot on our heels.

Without responding, Colin ran. When we entered the lobby, I knew we were home free. We were going to make it! A grin spread across my face. I looked at Colin, and he was grinning too.

Suddenly a dark shadow slid out from the side hall and skidded across the floor in front of us. My grin disappeared. Colin stopped dead in his tracks, and I ran into his back with a thump. Dr. Girard. How could he have gotten in front of us?

Seeing the shocked looks on our faces, Dr. Girard grinned. "There are lots of things you kids don't know about this old factory."

The sound of pounding feet stopped behind us. I

turned and saw Mr. Finnigan blocking the hallway to the offices and archives. We were trapped. Unless ... I looked out onto the crowded factory floor filled with old bottling machines and shadows. The same floor where my Great-Grandfather Patterson had worked every day because he'd sold his only daughter to his boss.

Dr. Girard grinned. "Hand over the briefcase, and you can go home."

"No way!" Colin fired back.

"Forget it," I added. I lightly tapped Colin on the shoulder and whispered, "Follow me."

Dr. Girard slowly approached us from the front and Mr. Finnigan from the back.

"Kids, this is all a big misunderstanding," Mr. Finnigan said. "I'm sure we can work something out—a compromise that will satisfy us all."

"You could have had a compromise a long time ago." I grabbed the back of Colin's shirt and pulled him and the briefcase onto the factory floor.

We ran among the mammoth-sized machines, assembly lines, and bottle washers. I heard Dr. Girard shout in rage as we disappeared.

Colin and I crouched low as we wove in and out of the machines. "We have to find somewhere to hide until we can make a clean break and run for our bikes," I whispered.

Colin wheezed back, unable to speak. I grabbed his hand and pulled him deeper into the labyrinth of metal. Even after all these decades of disuse, the floor smelled faintly of gasoline and maybe a hint of spilt ginger ale.

I found the perfect spot under one of the conveyor belts. It went all the way down to the floor but had an opening just big enough for the two of us to crawl underneath. "Here, you go first."

Colin stared back at me, his eyes as wide as saucers. His chest heaved up and down as he gasped for air. "Do you have your inhaler?" I asked.

He shook his head.

This wasn't good. He began wheezing more loudly.

I heard footsteps approaching. "You can't hide in here forever!" Dr. Girard cried. "Just give me the briefcase and then you can leave."

Colin started to tremble, his wheezing worsened by the second.

"In and out," I said to him. "Slowly, in and out."

The footsteps were right beside us on the closed side of the conveyor belt.

Colin clutched his hand to his chest. I couldn't hear Dr. Girard any longer. But then his voice boomed from right above us. "I know you're under there. I can hear Colin breathing."

The dim light seeping through the cracks in the assembly line illuminated Colin's face. I grimaced as it slowly turned an ugly shade of purple. Andora wouldn't want this to happen.

I heard a scraping noise on the cement floor, and then the small hole of light that Colin and I had crawled through disappeared. I released Colin's hand and crawled over to the space. A piece of sheet metal was now covering the opening. Dr. Girard must have moved it there to block our only way out. I tried to move it, but the sharp edge cut my hand. I felt a thin trail of blood flow down my wrist and onto my arm. I pounded against the metal. "Let us out! Colin is sick! He needs a doctor!"

"The briefcase first," Dr. Girard said, his voice muffled.

My eyes finally adjusted to the lack of light, and I looked back at Colin. He shook his head back and forth. His body was shaking, fighting for air.

"We have to."

Colin shook his head again.

I crawled back over to him. "Colin, please." He clutched the briefcase even tighter in his arms. "Do it for Andora. She wouldn't want you to die this way. Just think: if you die, who's going to go with me to meet her and tell her who she really is? You don't want her to find out about this when Dr. Girard's book is published, do you?"

Slowly, Colin loosened his grip on the case, and I pried the handle from his fingers. I crawled back to the opening. "I have it!" I shouted. Sweat poured down my face and into my eyes. This was all my fault. Why had I ever thought we could hide on the factory floor? After all of those hours of research, Dr. Girard knew every nook and cranny of the museum.

"Excellent. I'll slide the panel open, and you push the briefcase out to me."

"Okay."

Slowly, the light moved in. The opening was just big enough for the briefcase, and I pushed it through. But as soon as the briefcase went out, the panel slipped back into place. I pounded on the sharp metal, "Hey! Let us out!"

Dr. Girard's voice sounded close, as if he were kneeling right beside me. And his tone made my skin crawl. "What you need is discipline, young lady. And since I doubt that nutty aunt of yours is going to deliver it, I'll let you two stew for a little while longer."

"Let us out! You got what you wanted. Colin needs a doctor."

"Nice acting."

"Mr. Finnigan!" I cried, pounding on the metal. "Mr. Finnigan! Please help us! Colin is having an asthma attack. Please!"

I looked back at Colin whose whole body now heaved up and down, up and down. I heard Dr. Girard stand up and walk away. I crawled back to Colin and held his hand. He clasped mine with all his strength.

"It will be okay. It will be okay."

And then I prayed with all my might. It was the first prayer I'd offered since my parents died. "Please, God, not again. Please don't do this to me again. Help Colin. Please."

A loud bang followed by some scuffling sounds came from the other side of the metal panel. I crawled back over to it, and in a moment the panel slid out of view and the light streamed in. I rushed back to Colin and pulled him toward the opening. "Come on!"

We crawled outside.

Mr. Finnigan, tousled and red-faced, stood on the other side. "Bring him out." He had a cell phone in one hand, and in the other hand he held a steaming cup of coffee. "We have a boy here at the museum who's having an asthma attack. Hurry!" he said into the phone, and then he knelt down and handed me the paper coffee cup. "Give this to him; it will clear his airway."

"But …"

"Just do it!"

I put the coffee to Colin's mouth, and without hesitation he drank a big gulp of it. He coughed and sputtered. After a few more gulps, he was still wheezing, but he wasn't shaking as badly. I leaned him against a nearby machine.

I heard the sound of sirens getting closer. Mr. Finnigan left the factory floor to go meet the paramedics. I stood up and saw Dr. Girard lying on the floor. He was rubbing the top of his head, looking dazed. I grabbed an old monkey wrench off the floor nearby and walked over to Dr. Girard. The wrench was part of the new tool display that Mr. Finnigan had been planning.

"Don't move," I said.

"I don't intend to," Dr. Girard muttered.

Mr. Finnigan and the paramedics ran into the room and knelt beside Colin. He was still struggling to breathe. A female paramedic rummaged through her medical bag and pulled out a vial and a syringe. Colin's eyes went wide, but he was too out-of-breath to object. I turned away when the woman pushed up Colin's sleeve and stuck the needle into his upper arm. I wanted to run over and make absolutely sure that Colin was all right, but I glanced back down at Dr. Girard. There was no way I was letting him out of my sight.

When two police officers ran in just seconds later, it felt like hours had passed. I was still pointing the monkey wrench at Dr. Girard, who now sat cross-legged on the dusty cement floor and gingerly rubbed the large goose egg on the back of his head.

Dr. Girard was nobody's fool, and he immediately said, "Officers, thank goodness you're here. I suggest you take that weapon away from the girl." Dr. Girard's voice commanded authority.

The young officer was no match for Dr. Girard's tone. "Hand me the wrench," he said, giving me what I suspected was his sternest glower. I gave him the wrench.

Dr. Girard stood up while supporting his head with his left hand. He faltered a bit. The second police officer, a tall middle-aged man, grabbed the professor's arm to support him. Dr. Girard shook him off. "Take that girl into custody."

The young officer took hold of my arm. His name tag read, Officer Harrison.

I pulled away from him. "I didn't do anything wrong."

Mr. Finnigan jumped up and joined us. "Let go of her." But Mr. Finnigan's voice wasn't half as intimidating as Dr. Girard's. So Officer Harrison didn't release me. Mr. Finnigan stood beside me, but I stepped as far away from him as I could while the officer still restrained me. I felt him watching me, but I refused to meet his eyes. Then Mr. Finnigan swallowed and said, "Andi didn't do anything wrong. I'm the one you want."

Dr. Girard arrogantly tossed his head back and then winced with pain. He pointed at Mr. Finnigan. "He's the one who struck me. I want him arrested for assault."

Out of the corner of my eye, I saw Mr. Finnigan's lower lip quiver, and I felt a twinge of sympathy in my chest. But then I remembered how he'd used Colin and me. And how he'd used Andora.

The officers looked from Mr. Finnigan to Dr. Girard and back again. "Is that true?"

"Yes," Mr. Finnigan whispered. Officer Harrison released his hold on my arm and grasped the curator's arm instead. In one fluid movement, he pulled a pair of handcuffs from his utility belt and snapped them onto Mr. Finnigan's wrists with a clack.

"Wait!" I cried.

The officers gave me their full attention again.

I searched for the right words. "Yes, Mr. Finnigan hit Dr. Girard on the head. But he only did it to save us. Dr. Girard trapped Colin and me under that conveyor belt and wouldn't let us out." I pointed toward the sheet of metal and then held up my injured hand as evidence. The cut was now a clotted dark crease across my palm. Seeing it for the first time, I felt the pain of it shoot up my arm.

Dr. Girard rolled his eyes. "Nonsense."

"You trapped us under there while Colin was having an asthma attack."

Officer Harrison raised an eyebrow dubiously. "Why would he do that?"

I took a deep breath. "He wanted Andora's story. I learned about her when I found a trunk in my attic, but Dr. Girard was already writing a book about her. When he learned that Colin and I were searching for her too, he tried to trick us into helping him. When we wouldn't do it, he convinced Mr. Finnigan to steal Miss Addy's journal from us."

Dr. Girard shook his head and smiled at the officers, as if to say, "What an imagination this girl has!"

The officers didn't smile back.

Dr. Girard paled. "You're going to believe her story?"

"I have proof!" I cried. "Where's the briefcase?" I'd forgotten all about it during the commotion.

"What briefcase?" Dr. Girard asked.

"You know what I'm talking about."

Out of the corner of my eye, I saw movement. I looked over at Colin, who couldn't speak because an oxygen mask covered his face, and I saw he was waving at me. He pointed where the corner of the briefcase was sticking out from behind the conveyor belt.

"It's there ..."

The officer holding Dr. Girard's arm looked behind him. "I see it."

I ran over and grabbed the case. I released the clasp and riffled through the contents until I found Miss Addy's journal. It was still there wrapped in brown paper. Lovingly, I opened the journal and flipped through the pages. It was undisturbed. I rose and held up the book for the policemen to see. "This is the journal." Then I looked Mr. Finnigan in the eye. "And Mr. Finnigan stole it from my house."

"You see," Dr. Girard said, "I'm not to blame. It's him."

"He stole it *for* you," I snapped.

Mr. Finnigan, who so far had remained quiet during my tale, said, "Everything she said is true. Dr. Girard is obsessed with the connection between the Pike and Boggs families. He used me—no, I *let him* use me to get close to the children, to find out what they knew. I didn't think he would hurt them. I never thought they'd be in danger."

The tall officer roughly pulled Dr. Girard's arms behind him and yanked his handcuffs out of his utility belt. "Let's take them both to the station and sort this out."

Officer Harrison held out his hand toward me. "You're going to have to give us the briefcase and journal for evidence." At my anxious look, he smiled. "Don't worry. We'll make sure the journal is returned to Miss Addy unharmed."

I rewrapped the journal in its paper cover and slipped it back into the briefcase. Reluctantly, I handed the case to Officer Harrison.

Dr. Girard jerked his arms away, but the officer held fast and clamped the cuffs on his wrists in a practiced motion.

"I didn't know the boy was sick."

That could be true, I thought. But lies slipped so easily off of Dr. Girard's tongue, I would never know for sure.

"So you admit you trapped the children under there?" The tall officer asked, gesturing toward the conveyor belt.

Dr. Girard's eyes widened as he realized his mistake. "These kids don't appreciate history like I do. They can't make it come alive and make people care about it like I can."

"But I do appreciate it because it's *my history*. Not yours," I said.

"I still want to press assault charges," Dr. Girard growled.

"We'll talk about it at the station, sir." The tall officer pulled him toward the exit.

Dr. Girard dragged his heels on the cement floor, but there was no friction on the smooth surface to slow his progress. Panic filled his voice, "I didn't know the boy was sick. I thought the girl was joking. I tell you, I didn't know!"

Unfazed, the tall officer said, "See you at the station, Pete."

Officer Harrison nodded, and after Dr. Girard was out of sight, he pulled Mr. Finnigan in the direction of the exit as well. "Can I make sure Colin is all right before we leave?" Mr. Finnigan asked.

Officer Harrison nodded.

One of the paramedics packed up their gear, and the other one helped Colin into a wheelchair. The female paramedic smiled when she saw my worried look. "It's just a precaution. He should be fine. We're taking him to the clinic for a full checkup. We've already called his grandma and your aunt. They'll meet us at the clinic. Want to ride along in the ambulance?"

"Sure," I said. I grinned at Colin. He grinned back, pale-faced, but eyes gleaming.

Colin pulled the oxygen mask from his face and rasped, "We saved the journal."

"We did," I agreed. "We make a good team."

Colin beamed but then started coughing dry, hoarse coughs in rapid succession.

"You're sure he's all right?" Mr. Finnigan looked forlorn with his hands cuffed behind his back.

"He'll be fine. The coffee you gave him really made the difference. That shot of caffeine was enough to slow down the attack. It saved his life."

Colin gave Mr. Finnigan a weak smile from behind the oxygen mask.

The paramedics wheeled Colin toward the exit, and I moved to follow. I stole a glance at Mr. Finnigan as he watched them go. He swallowed hard and seemed to sense my gaze. I looked away and started to follow the paramedics.

Mr. Finnigan made a choking sound. "Andi! Wait! I'm—I'm sorry."

"It's okay," I said automatically, not because I forgave him, but because it seemed like the polite thing to do.

"No, it's not. Dr. Girard didn't care about this museum, the historical society, or about anyone other than himself. He cared only for his career. I should have known this before. Deep down, I did know. But with the museum failing, I wanted to believe his lies.

"When you kids were under the conveyor belt, it felt as if someone slapped me awake and made me realize the truth about Dr. Girard all at once. So I grabbed the wrench out of the box and hit him with it."

I put my hand on his arm. "It's okay, Mr. Finnigan," I said, really meaning it this time. "You saved Colin's life. That's all that matters now."

"It's time to go," Officer Harrison said.

Colin and I beat Amelie and Bergita to the clinic, thanks to the ambulance's siren and flashing lights, but only by a few seconds. Amelie reached us first. Her face was pale under her deep summer tan.

"Andi!" she cried and grabbed me into a bear hug, not unlike the one she'd given me on the day Bethany and I moved to Killdeer.

Underneath her hug, I felt my aunt trembling. With my face smushed into her side, I couldn't answer her. Her hold on me made my lips press painfully against my braces.

"Oh, for crying out loud, let the girl breathe," Bergita said.

Amelie released me. "I'm sorry. Are you hurt?"

Behind her, I was surprised to see my sister standing there. Bethany's eye makeup was smudged as if she'd been crying. She ran up to me. "How could you be so stupid? You could have gotten hurt!" Tears sprung to her eyes.

"I ... I'm sorry, Bethany."

She folded her arms. "Don't do it again." Then she crushed me in a hug that was brief but twice as strong as Amelie's.

Bergita scowled down at Colin. "Am I to understand that you left the house without your inhaler, young man?"

Colin's grin vanished. "I ... I forgot."

Bergita stiffened. "You give me another scare like that, and you're not leaving the house for a month. You understand me?"

"Yes, Grandma."

It was the first time I'd heard Colin call Bergita by that name.

Bergita gave him a crooked smile, leaned over, and gave her grandson a huge hug to rival any that Amelie could dish out.

Amelie put her hands on her hips and tried to look stern. "Andi, you are double grounded now."

"What does double grounded mean?"

"I haven't decided yet." Amelie wrapped her arms around Bethany and me. "So, are you going to tell me what you discovered?"

I happily obliged, and Colin jumped in every so often with any details I'd forgotten.

EPILOGUE

The night before we were to meet Andora in person, Amelie asked if she could invite Mr. Finnigan to come along. "Mr. Finnigan is a good man, Andi," she said. "I want to you to remember that. He just wanted so badly to save the museum. But he learned his lesson—the hard way. Adults still have a lot to learn, too." Her eyebrows dipped in concern. "I'm sure your dad would have explained this to you better."

I gently bumped my shoulder against hers. "You're doing all right. Mr. Finnigan could have found another way to save the museum." I paused. "But he should still come. He knows Andora's story better than anyone."

Amelie smiled. "That's a very mature decision. Your mom and dad would be proud of you—even if you are double grounded."

The next day, I sat between Bethany and Colin in the backseat of Amelie's Jeep, heading north up Interstate 77 toward Akron.

Back in Killdeer, I knew Dr. Girard would be cleaning out his office in the History Department under Wally's watchful eyes. Amelie told me Michael Pike University had fired him. But he wouldn't go to jail even though the police originally charged him with child endangerment. They dropped the charges when Dr. Girard dropped his assault charges against Mr. Finnigan.

Amelie said Dr. Girard's loss of tenure was the worst punishment they could have given him anyway.

Mr. Finnigan sat in the passenger seat next to my aunt, chatting with her about the book she was writing about the Boggs and Pike family histories. Mr. Finnigan wanted to help her with the research. And he was also helping Miss Addy publish her journals. I'd told her I wanted the first signed copy.

"How much longer?" Bethany whined.

Amelie glanced at us in the rearview mirror and made eye contact with me. I rolled my eyes and she smiled. "It will be another hour at least."

We were on our way to the small city of Hudson, which is just north of Akron, to visit Mrs. Peggy Pike Matthews—also known as known as Andora Felicity Boggs. She knew the whole story—her story—by now. After the initial shock had subsided, she'd invited us to her home to have lunch with her. Her two children (Amelie's cousins) and their children—my second cousins—would be there as well. I had cousins!

I rubbed my sweaty hands up and down my shorts. Colin glanced over at me. "So this one's in the bag? The case, I mean."

"Yeah, it is."

"So I guess Boggs and Carter Investigations is now out of business," he said glumly.

I looked over and grinned. "No way. We're just on hiatus until another mystery comes along."

Colin grinned back. "And that could happen any day."

ACKNOWLEDGEMENT

When I was a little girl, my Irish grandfather, Albert Martin, used to entertain my brother and me with stories about his life during the Great Depression and the Second World War. That's where my fascination with the time period began. And when I was an adult, those stories sparked the idea for *Andi Unexpected*, a novel I wrote simply because I loved the story. I never expected it to be published.

However, when I told my agent, Nicole Resciniti, that I had a children's book saved on my computer, she asked to see it and said with certainty that it would be published. As always, she was right. I thank her for constantly believing in my work and in me—even when I don't.

I'm also grateful to Zondervan and my wonderful editor, Kim Childress, who saw a place for Andi and me on their bookshelves. I'm honored to work with you.

Thanks also to dear friends Mariellyn Grace and Melody Steiner who read this manuscript so many years ago.

Love to my parents Thomas Flower, who is in heaven, and Reverend Pamela Flower, who read this manuscript countless times. You gave my brother and me a childhood full of laughter and adventure. Without that, I would not have been able to write this novel.

And finally, I thank God in heaven because every dream that comes true is larger than I expected it to be.

Talk It Up!

Want free books?
First looks at the best new fiction?
Awesome exclusive merchandise?

We want to hear from you!

Give us your opinions on titles, covers, and stories.
Join the Z Street Team.

Visit zstreetteam.zondervan.com/joinnow
to sign up today!

Also—Friend us on Facebook!

www.facebook.com/goodteenreads

- Video Trailers
- Connect with your favorite authors
- Sneak peeks at new releases
- Giveaways
- Fun discussions
- And much more!